Deadly
Cruise Ship Christ
Series Book 14

Hope Callaghan

*****

hopecallaghan.com
Copyright © 2018
All rights reserved.

This book is a work of fiction. Although places mentioned may be real, the characters, names and incidents, and all other details are products of the author's imagination and are fictitious. Any resemblance to actual organizations, events, or actual persons, living or dead is purely coincidental.

No part of this publication may be copied, reproduced in any format, by any means, electronic or otherwise, without prior consent from the copyright owner and publisher of this book.

Visit my website for new releases and special offers: hopecallaghan.com

Thank you to these wonderful ladies who help make my books shine - Peggy H., Cindi G., Jean P., Wanda D., Barbara W. and Renate P. for taking the time to preview *Deadly Delivery*, for the extra sets of eyes and for catching all of my mistakes.

A special THANKS to my reader review teams, here in the U.S., and those across the pond, over the border and an ocean away!

Alice, Amary, Barbara, Becky, Brinda, Cassie, Charlene, Christina, Debbie, Dee, Denota, Devan, Grace, Jan, Jo-Ann, Joyce, Jean K., Jean M., Katherine, Lynne, Megan, Melda, Kat, Linda, Lynne, Pat, Patsy, Paula, Rebecca, Rita, Tamara, Valerie, Vicki and Virginia.

Allie, Anca, Angela, Ann, Anne, Bev, Bobbi, Bonny, Carol, Carmen, David, Debbie, Diana, Elaine, Elizabeth, Gareth, Ingrid, Jane, Jayne, Jean, Joan, Karen, Kate, Kathy, Lesley, Margaret, Marlene, Patricia, Pauline, Sharon, Sheila and Susan.

Thank you to Marcia Lamb for submitting her recipe, Pumpkin Crunch Cake – Kauai Style!

CONTENTS

CAST OF CHARACTERS IV
CHAPTER 1 1
CHAPTER 2 16
CHAPTER 3 34
CHAPTER 4 49
CHAPTER 5 64
CHAPTER 6 73
CHAPTER 7 87
CHAPTER 8 100
CHAPTER 9 112
CHAPTER 10 130
CHAPTER 11 142
CHAPTER 12 161
CHAPTER 13 176
CHAPTER 14 189
CHAPTER 15 205
CHAPTER 16 216
CHAPTER 17 228
CHAPTER 18 245
CHAPTER 19 257
CHAPTER 20 273
CHAPTER 21 289
CHAPTER 22 303
BOOKS IN THIS SERIES 311
MEET THE AUTHOR 312
PUMPKIN CRUNCH CAKE RECIPE 314

Cast of Characters

Mildred Sanders. Mildred "Millie" Sanders, heartbroken after her husband left her for one of his clients, decides to take a position as assistant cruise director aboard the mega cruise ship, Siren of the Seas. From day one, she discovers she has a knack for solving mysteries, which is a good thing since some sort of crime is always being committed on the high seas.

Annette Delacroix. Director of Food and Beverage on board Siren of the Seas, Annette has a secret past and is the perfect accomplice in Millie's investigations. Annette is the "Jill of all Trades" and isn't afraid to roll up her sleeves and help out her friend in need.

Catherine "Cat" Wellington. Cat is the most cautious of the group of friends and prefers to help Millie from the sidelines. But when push comes to shove, Cat can be counted on to risk life and limb in the pursuit of justice.

Danielle Kneldon. Millie's former cabin mate. Headstrong and gung ho, Danielle loves a good adventure and loves physical challenges, including scaling the side of the ship, scouring the jungles of Central America and working undercover to solve a mystery.

Then Jesus said to his disciples, "Therefore I tell you, do not worry about your life, what you will eat; or about your body, what you will wear. For life is more than food, and the body more than clothes. Consider the ravens: They do not sow or reap, they have no storeroom or barn; yet God feeds them. And how much more valuable you are than birds! Who of you by worrying can add a single hour to your life? Luke 12:22-25 NIV

Chapter 1

Millie smoothed the burnt orange leaf, shifted the pinecone, and took a step back to admire the festive fall garland. "I hate to admit it, but Andy's fall decorations are perfect."

"Agreed, but don't you think he's going a tad overboard with the fall festival theme?" Annette asked. "He's in my kitchen every day asking me how the fall menu is shaping up. If he had his way, we would all be eating pumpkin bisque, pumpkin pie, pumpkin pancakes."

Millie smiled. "You can thank the Baroness of the Seas' cruise director, Claudia, for Andy's new obsession."

Ever since the Baroness joined the ship's fleet, Andy and Claudia bantered back and forth, each claiming they were the number one cruise director. Andy and Claudia had recently engaged in a fall-themed wager, starting with the September cruises and ending on Thanksgiving Day.

The friendly competition was based on passenger comment cards...the ship and/or cruise director who received the largest number of positive comments, directly related to their fall theme, would win. Andy and Claudia had even enlisted the help of the corporate activity coordinator to track and count the comments.

"So what's in it for the winner?" Annette asked.

"I have no idea and I don't think it matters. Andy is determined we're going to win this contest. He has a whole slew of fall trinkets waiting to be picked up in Miami tomorrow."

"That oughta make Sharky happy, having to haul all of the extra boxes on board the ship." Annette glanced at her watch. "I better get going. I need to check on the cakes and scones for this afternoon's formal tea."

Millie followed Annette out of the atrium and up to deck seven. "I need to get a move on, too. I'm hosting a speed painting competition in the theater."

"The contestants will probably be painting pumpkins." Annette chuckled and waved good-bye to her friend before stepping inside the galley.

When Millie reached the theater, the participants were already forming a line. It snaked along the front of the stage and down the center aisle.

Millie met Danielle near the front. "It looks like we're going to have a big turnout. I had no idea this many people would be interested in speed painting."

Because of the large turnout, the women decided to host two segments. Millie briefly explained the rules of the game to the participants while Danielle fiddled with the music soundboard to find some snappy tunes.

More passengers began filtering in to watch the contestants create a seaside landscape. Millie circled the stage and admired the artwork, impressed by both the speed and talent of the guests on board.

After finishing both rounds, the audience selected the winner and runner-up via applause, and Millie presented each of them with a ship on a stick and a café gift card.

Danielle waited until the theater was empty before making her way to the nearest easel and grabbing a handful of dirty paintbrushes. "That was fun."

"You should try it," Millie said.

"Nah. Painting requires too much concentration and attention to detail. If I were to take up a hobby, it would be digging for gold. I've always been fascinated with treasure hunters."

"I'll have to remember that." Millie followed Danielle and began folding easels. "How's it going with your new cabin mate?"

"It's not." Danielle wrinkled her nose. "She's lazy, messy, not to mention rude and those are her positive traits."

"You need to give her a chance. She just moved in." Danielle had been enjoying having the cabin to herself after Millie, who had been Danielle's cabin mate, married Captain Armati and moved out.

Millie secretly suspected Danielle thought Andy and Donovan Sweeney forgot she was the only one occupying the cabin. She warned her young friend it was only a matter of time before someone moved in and Danielle was none too happy the day Tonya arrived on her doorstep.

According to Danielle, she waltzed in acting as if she owned the place and rattled off her list of demands, which included an afternoon rest time to nap in between work shifts and insisting she not be disturbed.

Danielle forgot and stopped by to charge her cell phone, waking Tonya during her naptime and the two argued. The argument set the tone for their relationship and Danielle claimed she couldn't stand the woman.

"Tonya's afternoon naps are morphing into sleeping in late, working short shifts, and then it's back to bed until her afternoon shift. After dark, she's out partying all night and stumbling home in the wee hours of the morning."

"It sounds as if Tonya might not work out. Maybe you should ask Donovan and Andy to find you a different cabin mate."

"I already have." Danielle sighed heavily. "There's nowhere for her to go and we don't have another crew changeover until December, so I'm stuck with her. When I left this morning, her lazy butt was still in bed. If she keeps it up, she'll get canned and then I won't have to worry about it."

"I'm sorry." Millie patted Danielle's arm. "If it gets too bad, you're welcome to sleep on our sofa bed."

"Thanks for the offer." Danielle smiled gratefully. "I may take you up on it, but then you won't be able to get rid of me."

The women finished storing the painting supplies and began walking down the center aisle to the lobby. "How's it going with Andy's fall project?"

"Oh brother." Millie rolled her eyes. "He's all in on this competition with Claudia. He told me he's finishing up his whole fall themed schedule of events and is planning a special staff meeting Saturday morning to go over the schedule."

"He's already warned me I'll be helping out with the Siren Sailors, the eight to twelve year-olds," Danielle said.

"Doing what?"

"Trick or treating, apple bobbing. He's even talking about assembling a haunted house in the game room."

"That sounds like fun."

Millie's radio squawked. "Millie, do you copy?" It was Andy.

She lifted the radio. "Go ahead, Andy."

"Where are you?"

"I just finished co-hosting speed painting with Danielle. What's up?"

"Perfect. I need to have a quick meeting with both of you in Donovan's office."

"We're on our way." Millie clipped the radio to her belt. "I wonder what that's all about."

"Andy probably wants to make sure he gets his boxes of goodies delivered and is going to put us in charge of decorating." Danielle led the way to Donovan's office, located behind the guest services desk. She rapped lightly on his office door before sticking her head around the corner.

Donovan Sweeney, the ship's purser, motioned the women inside. "Thanks for getting down here on short notice."

Andy turned. "We have a small crisis."

"What kind of crisis?" Millie settled into an empty chair next to Andy and Danielle joined her on the other side.

"Josh's mother is in hospice now," Donovan replied. "He's getting off the ship tomorrow. We're not sure if he'll be returning."

Millie let out a small gasp. "Oh no. That's terrible news. Poor Josh." She and the other entertainment staff started a *GoFundMe* page for Josh and his family after the young crewmember confided in

Millie and Andy that his mother had been diagnosed with cancer. He was sending his paycheck home to help pay the bills.

"We met with Josh, and he knows he's welcome to rejoin the Siren of the Seas when or if he wants to," Donovan said.

"In the meantime, we'll be a little short staffed. The fall festivities will continue as planned," Andy said. "In fact, I called the port this morning and all of the boxes have arrived and are waiting to be loaded as soon as we dock."

"Perfect." Danielle snapped her fingers. "Can you move Tonya into Josh's empty bunk?"

"Danielle," Andy chided. "This feuding between you and Tonya needs to stop. First you complain about her, and then she files a complaint against you..."

"You're kidding! That witch had the nerve to file a complaint against *me?* For what?"

"She claims you're harassing her."

Danielle sprang from the chair. "Where's the complaint? I have a right to see a copy."

Andy and Donovan exchanged an uneasy glance and Andy nodded. "She has a right to see it."

Donovan reached into his desk drawer and pulled out a file folder. He slid it across the desk. "You and I need to sit down and discuss this calmly."

"We'll see about that." Danielle snatched the file folder off the desk and flipped it open. "Unauthorized visitors, tampering with Tonya's personal belongings…" There was a long moment of silence. "Theft?" She looked up, her eyes wide. "She accused me of stealing from her?"

"Oh dear," Millie muttered. "Surely, you don't believe Danielle would steal from another employee."

Donovan ran a ragged hand through his hair. "My job is to take each and every employee complaint seriously. I'm sorry, Danielle. If you wish to file a counter-complaint, we can handle it after our meeting with Andy and Millie."

"You better believe it. That's exactly what I plan to do." Danielle slammed the folder shut and dropped it on the desk. "Just as soon as I give the liar a piece of my mind."

Danielle was halfway to the door when she abruptly stopped and slowly turned. "Wait a minute...I'm sure you've already written Tonya up for showing up late for her shift today. She was still in bed when I left the cabin this morning."

"Are you sure?" Donovan turned his attention to his computer. "I'm checking the employee schedule and don't see anything. Tonya works in spa services. Let me call the spa manager."

Donovan picked up his phone. "Hello, Camille. Donovan Sweeney here. I'm calling to inquire about one of your employees, Tonya Rivera. Is she working today?"

There was a brief pause while Donovan listened. "I see. What time?"

He thanked the woman on the other end and then told her good-bye. "Tonya isn't working this morning. Camille said her first appointment isn't for another hour, so she had the morning off."

"Good. Then it won't be hard to track her down." Danielle grabbed the doorknob.

"Danielle." The hard edge in Andy's voice stopped Danielle. "I know you're upset and with good reason, but you need to calm down. As Donovan said, he has to investigate Tonya's claim. Millie can vouch for you, having been your cabin mate for a long time."

Millie wiggled out of her chair and made her way to her co-worker's side. "Andy is right. Confronting Tonya will only make matters worse. Why don't we go to your cabin and pack some of your clothes? You can stay with Nic and me until things settle down."

Danielle's shoulders slumped and she nodded her head. "Thanks, Millie. I think I will take you up on the offer."

"That's definitely an upgrade in accommodations," Andy joked. "In the meantime, Donovan and I will try to work on getting Tonya transferred to a different cabin."

The relief on Danielle's face was clearly visible. "Thanks, Andy. I owe you one."

Millie followed Danielle out of Donovan's office. "We'll grab some of your things and if we're lucky, Tonya won't be there."

"If she is, I'm going to bite my tongue," Danielle promised. "I'm so glad Andy finally agreed to move her."

When they reached Danielle's cabin, she slipped her keycard in the slot and slowly pushed the door open. The room was dark, and she fumbled for the light switch.

Millie sniffed the air. "What's that awful smell?"

"Who knows? Rotting food, dirty laundry," Danielle whispered. "Like I said, my cabin mate isn't the tidiest."

Bright light illuminated the small cabin and it took a moment for Millie's eyes to adjust. Her eyes were drawn to the upper bunk, where someone lay sleeping.

"Disgusting." Danielle marched across the cabin and tapped the young woman's arm. "Hey, wake up sleeping beauty. It's nearly noon."

"Danielle," Millie shook her head. "Let's just grab your stuff and go."

"Fine." Danielle spun on her heel and headed to the closet while Millie stared at the woman's still form. Something was wrong.

Millie inched forward. Waves of jet-black hair swirled around the woman's head, forming a halo. "Tonya." She gently nudged the woman's arm.

There was no movement. It was then Millie noticed the woman wasn't breathing.

Chapter 2

"Danielle."

"Yeah, hang on, I'm almost ready. I'm trying to be quiet."

"There's no need." Millie's eyes were transfixed on Tonya. Now that she really looked, the woman's face was tranquil and peaceful. She fumbled with her radio and shifted her attention to Danielle, who was still rummaging through a drawer.

"Dave Patterson, do you copy?"

"Go ahead, Millie."

"I need you to come to C224, Danielle Kneldon's cabin, as soon as possible."

"I'm in a meeting."

Millie interrupted. "It's kind of important."

There was a brief pause. "I'm on my way."

Millie set her walkie-talkie on the desk and grabbed the cabin phone's receiver. Her finger shook as she dialed the number for the medical center.

"What's going on?" Danielle dropped her bag and approached Tonya's bunk. She tugged on the corner of the sheet and slowly pulled it down. "Uh-oh."

Millie closed her eyes and prayed that Gundervan was around. She didn't want to have to call him on the radio, knowing that anyone listening in would realize something serious had happened after summoning Dave Patterson, the head of security and then the ship's doctor.

Rachel, the ship's nurse, answered. "Medical Center. Rachel Quaid speaking."

"Yes. This is Millie Armati. Is Doctor Gundervan around?"

"Hold on a sec." Millie could hear muffled sounds before Rachel returned to the call. "What's going on?" she demanded.

"You'll find out soon enough. I need to speak with Gundervan."

"Fine." After another muffled sound, Doctor Gundervan answered. "Doctor Gundervan speaking."

"Yes, this is Millie Armati. I'm in employee cabin two twenty-four...Danielle Kneldon's cabin. Her roommate is in her bunk and unresponsive. I think she's dead."

"Have you checked for a pulse?"

"No. I haven't." Millie made a move to return to the bunk, but Danielle beat her to it and applied pressure to Tonya's neck. She shook her head. "No pulse."

"Danielle just checked. She has no pulse. Judging by her color, I think she's been...gone for some time."

"I'm on my way." Gundervan disconnected the line and Millie replaced the receiver.

"I swear she was alive when I left this morning." Danielle took a step back. "I mean, I can't be certain, but I thought she was stirring when I left."

"What time did you leave?"

"Around six, which is when I normally leave the cabin to start my workday. I can't believe this. Do you know how this looks?" Danielle's voice rose an octave as the realization she would be the prime suspect sank in.

"Don't panic yet, Danielle. She may have died of natural causes," Millie said.

Before the young woman could answer, there was a sharp rap on the door.

Millie hurried to open it and motioned Dave Patterson inside. She started to close the door when she spotted Doctor Gundervan striding down the long hall.

"Thank you for getting here so fast." Millie waited for Gundervan to step inside before explaining that when Danielle and she first arrived, they assumed Tonya was asleep.

"While Danielle was packing her things, I noticed Tonya wasn't moving, so I kinda nudged her arm." Millie watched as the doctor began checking Tonya's vitals.

"The crewmember is deceased. Based on my preliminary observations, there doesn't appear to be any visible trauma."

The men discussed removing Tonya's body and transporting it to the ship's morgue. "We'll need some help." Patterson called down to his office and soon, the cramped cabin was swarming with security personnel.

Donovan Sweeney arrived a short time later, followed by Andy and finally Millie's husband, Captain Armati.

Millie's claustrophobia kicked in and she excused herself to wait in the hall. Danielle joined her. "Seriously, I'm sure Tonya was still alive when I left."

"Is this the first time you've been back to the cabin since leaving first thing this morning?" Millie asked.

"Yeah. I didn't want to run into Tonya again, so I've been avoiding going home except to sleep." Danielle closed her eyes and leaned her head against the hall wall. "I wanted Tonya gone, but not like this."

The women watched as the security crew removed Tonya's body. Several more crewmembers followed behind, carrying a stack of dirty dishes along with several more items.

Patterson appeared in the doorway and motioned the women back inside.

Millie's stomach churned as she gazed at Tonya's empty bunk. A young woman was dead. There was no way Millie believed Danielle was responsible for the woman's death. Still, the circumstances didn't look good.

Patterson began questioning Danielle about the timeline, when she left the cabin and the last time she spoke with Tonya. After questioning Danielle at length, he asked them to step back outside, so he could conduct a final search of the cabin.

"Of course," Danielle said. "I have nothing to hide."

"Let's go down to the crew mess hall and grab a drink," Millie said. "There's nothing we can do until Patterson is finished."

The crew mess hall was nearly empty. Millie poured a cup of coffee and Danielle grabbed a can of Diet Coke before making their way to a table in the corner.

Several other crewmembers passed by, and Millie recognized a couple of them. They were part of the crowd that had gathered in the hall and watched as the security guards carried Tonya's body from the cabin.

Danielle slowly sipped her soda, her expression pinched and her face pale. "Maybe she was partying last night and drank too much."

Millie studied her friend's face. "You mentioned a couple of days ago Tonya was seeing someone…what was his name?"

"Arvin something. I know who he is. I've never actually met him. Tonya never brought him to our place, at least not while I was there."

"Yet she talked about him," Millie prompted.

"No." Danielle shook her head. "I saw them down in the employee lounge one evening getting cozy. I asked Tonya about it later, if she was dating Arvin and she got very defensive. They were hanging with the party crowd and you know that's not my scene."

Danielle was a young person with an old soul. She gravitated towards the older crowd, which was one of the reasons Millie and she got along.

"I'm sure Patterson will question Arvin." Millie sipped her coffee and eyed her friend over the rim of the cup. "Are you still going to take me up on the offer to stay with Nic and me?"

"No." Danielle shook her head. "You know my background. Bodies don't bother me, never have, although I feel bad for disliking Tonya and now she's dead."

"You had no idea," Millie said softly. "Your disliking her didn't kill her."

"I know, but our last words to each other weren't pleasant and now I feel guilty."

"It happens to the best of us." Millie caught a glimpse of Dave Patterson as he stepped inside the dining room and she motioned him over.

"I've finished my search. We can chat here or in private back in your cabin."

"Here will work." Danielle shifted her chair to make room for Patterson. "Like I said, I have nothing to hide."

"Are you sure?"

"Yes, I mean, I know you didn't find anything implicating me. I'm completely innocent."

"Danielle." Patterson glanced around before sitting down. "Is there anything you would like to tell me?"

"No." Danielle frowned and shook her head. "I'll admit I didn't care for Tonya, we argued, she reported me for some stupid stuff which wasn't true. That doesn't mean I was ticked off enough to take her out."

Patterson slowly nodded. "Are you feeling all right?"

"No, I'm not," Danielle snapped. "My cabin mate is dead and you're looking at me like you're waiting for a confession." Forgetting they were in a public area, Danielle's voice echoed in the room.

"Perhaps we should have this conversation in a more private location," Millie suggested.

"Fine." Danielle abruptly stood, tipping her chair over in the process. It hit the floor with a loud bang.

"This is a crock." She marched out of the dining room.

By the time Patterson and Millie caught up with Danielle, she was inside the cabin, pacing back and forth.

Millie could almost feel Danielle's fury and cautiously made her way across the room. "Danielle. Patterson is only doing his job. You know that."

"I know. I'm upset and overreacted." Danielle waited until Patterson closed the door behind them. "I'm sorry. Why did you ask me if I was feeling okay? Did Brody tell you we were fighting or something? Because if he did, it's news to me."

"This has nothing to do with Brody." Patterson stuck his hand in his pocket and pulled out a brown prescription bottle. "Does this look familiar?"

"No." Danielle squinted her eyes. "I don't do drugs, not even the over-the-counter stuff."

"Danielle hardly ever takes an aspirin," Millie confirmed.

"I found this in your jacket pocket."

"My pocket?" Danielle gasped. "You're kidding and that's seriously not funny."

"It's no joke." Patterson held it up. "As you can see, the RX information is missing."

"I swear that is not mine. To prove it, I'm going down to the medical center right now and take a random drug test."

"Are you sure you want to do that?" Patterson asked.

"I most definitely do. Someone stuck the bottle in my pocket and I hate to speak ill of the dead, but the only person who could've put it there was Tonya."

"I'm assuming they'll be performing a drug test during the autopsy," Millie said.

"Of course. It's standard operating procedure." Patterson motioned toward the door. "I'm sorry,

Danielle. You, more than anyone, understand I'm just doing my job."

"I know and I'm not even worried because I know my drug test will come back negative."

Millie's wristwatch chimed, reminding her she was scheduled to host the afternoon tea. She trailed behind Patterson and Danielle. "I've got to get going. Call me if you need me, Danielle."

"Will do."

Millie stepped into the stairwell and climbed the steps, her thoughts on Tonya and her mysterious death.

It was only a matter of time before Patterson cleared Danielle. Perhaps the prescription bottle belonged to Tonya and she intentionally planted it in Danielle's pocket to get her into trouble.

It was the only plausible explanation. Millie was certain that once Danielle passed the drug test, Patterson would clear her of suspicion.

She pushed the unsettling thoughts from her mind and walked to *The Vine,* the Italian restaurant where she was hosting the afternoon tea. The teatime was one of several activities she'd volunteered to host since Andy was up to his eyeballs in fall festival planning.

She wandered into the room and stepped off to the side as she watched the greeter seat the guests. As soon as the guests were seated, another employee approached the table with a pot of tea.

Other servers followed behind carrying large silver trays laden with decadent treats. One of the servers stopped to offer Millie something to eat.

Her mouth watered as she perused the offerings. "These look delicious. What are they?"

The server pointed at the small sandwiches with the tip of his tongs. "We have cucumber sandwiches, buttermilk and cinnamon scones with clotted cream, egg salad sandwiches and ham and cheese croissants."

"I'll take a buttermilk scone and a cucumber sandwich."

"Excellent choice." He transferred the goodies from his tray to an empty plate. "You will join the guests?"

"Of course." Millie carried her plate to a nearby table. "Do you mind if I join you?"

"The more, the merrier." A man seated at the table scrambled to pull out Millie's chair. "You're the assistant cruise director."

"I am." Millie settled into her seat and reached for her napkin as another uniformed server poured her a cup of tea. "Are you enjoying your cruise?"

She kept the conversation light as she munched on the delicious treats and chatted with the passengers about their voyage. Andy was big on having the staff chat with guests to get feedback on both the good and the bad.

The recurring theme Millie heard time and again was disappointment in the limited number of excursions available on the islands they visited, all of which had been damaged by the recent hurricanes. Today was no different.

She gently reminded them that the islanders depended on the tourists and cruise ships. "The more people who come to visit the islands, the faster they're able to recover."

After wrapping up the afternoon tea, Millie hosted a round of bingo, followed by a quick stop by the *High Seas Art Gallery* to listen in on a Van Gogh presentation.

The presentation was the last event of the afternoon before Millie's early dinner break. Still full from indulging in the decadent afternoon tea treats, she headed upstairs.

Nic and Captain Vitale were on the bridge when she arrived. "How are we looking for port arrival tomorrow?"

"We're right on schedule," Nic said. "How is Danielle?"

"Not good. I'm going to check on her after I leave here. Patterson searched her cabin and found a prescription bottle in the pocket of her work jacket. Last time I saw her, she was on her way to the medical center for a random drug test."

"What do you think?" Nic asked.

"I know Danielle is innocent, the pill bottle wasn't hers and Patterson will clear her name." Millie paused. "Why someone would plant a pill bottle in Danielle's jacket is beyond me, unless someone was trying to get her into trouble."

"I'm sure it will all sort itself out," Nic said. "We've contacted Ms. Rivera's family. They're on their way to Miami. I'm meeting them tomorrow after we dock."

"What a sad situation," Millie glanced at the clock. "I better get back to work." She told Nic and the staff captain good-bye and then slipped down to the ship's gift shop to chat with her friend, Cat.

Fridays were typically one of the gift shop's busiest days and the day when they hosted the final "Blowout Sale." The place was swarming with bargain hunters, eager to pick up last minute souvenirs or gifts for family back home.

Reluctant to fight the crowds, Millie pulled her work schedule from her pocket to track down Danielle. She discovered her friend was working in the ship's library, not far from the store.

Although there were a few passengers perusing the bookshelves, it wasn't nearly as packed as the gift shop.

Millie waited for several passengers to finish returning borrowed books and they were alone. "Well? I'm sure you passed the drug test."

"Yep, with flying colors," Danielle confirmed. "While I was there, Patterson slipped up and I found out something very interesting about Tonya Rivera."

Chapter 3

"Tonya Rivera worked on board the Marquise of the Seas, one of Majestic Cruise Lines' other ships. She filed some sort of complaint and right after filing, was transferred to the Siren of the Seas, which is how I ended up with her as my cabin mate."

"You have no idea what the complaint was about?" Millie asked.

"Nope." Danielle crossed her arms. "Do you see a pattern here? She filed a complaint on the Marquise of the Seas…lo and behold…she isn't my cabin mate for more than a month and she files a complaint against me."

"I'm surprised Majestic Cruise Lines let her transfer to our ship."

"There was more in Patterson's report, but he wouldn't let me see it," Danielle sighed.

"Tonya never mentioned her previous job on the sister ship?"

"Nope. I knew she worked on the other ship and it struck me as odd that she transferred to our ship mid-contract."

Majestic Cruise Lines, like most other cruise lines, contracted with each employee to work a designated number of months. After the contract was up, the employee took an extended break, many times returning to their home country to spend time with family before beginning a new work contract, often on a different ship than the one they left.

"Keep your chin up, Danielle. I'm sure Patterson will get to the bottom of it."

Millie exited the library, making her way to Andy's office as she mulled over Tonya Rivera's job transfer and sudden death. She had met the young woman just once, and could only imagine how her family felt at the heartbreaking news of her passing, so far from home.

There was the possibility she had died of natural causes, but Millie suspected Patterson didn't think so. Otherwise, he wouldn't have taken the time to remove several items from the cabin, including dirty dishes.

If the empty prescription bottle belonged to Tonya, and Millie believed it did, where did she get it? Did she bring it on board with her? What if the young woman had overdosed?

Vowing to do a little digging around after her shift ended, Millie knocked lightly on Andy's office door before stepping inside.

She found her boss sitting at the conference table, his head down as he concentrated on a pile of papers in front of him.

When he heard Millie, he looked up, his reading glasses slipping down his nose. "How is Danielle?"

"Upset." Millie sank into an empty chair. "She feels guilty. She disliked Tonya and now the woman is dead."

"It's an unfortunate situation for everyone, most of all for the young woman's family." Andy repeated what Nic had already told her, that Tonya's family was on their way to Miami to meet with the investigators and the ship's officers.

Andy changed the subject. "I'm working on the fall festival youth activities. I scoped out the game room. It's the perfect spot to transform into a haunted house." He told Millie he'd already enlisted the help of several of the entertainment staff to set up and run the haunted house.

"Where do I fit into these fun fall festivities?"

"I'm glad you asked." Andy slid some papers across the desk. "The top two sheets list the stuff waiting at the port, and the bottom sheet is a list of activities."

"What about our regular activity schedule? Are we going to keep any of our regular schedule?"

"Some of it. We can't get rid of bingo since it's a big money maker. Instead of B-I-N-G-O numbers, I found a company who makes fall themed bingo cards. The call letters are G-H-O-S-T instead of bingo. Isn't it brilliant?" Andy beamed.

"Yeah," Millie chuckled. "It's a great idea."

He rattled on about the new activities as Millie scanned the list. Not only had Andy included a haunted house, there was a create-your-own-costume activity for the children, pumpkin drawing, apple bobbing and pumpkin piñatas.

"I'm still working on the adult activities." Andy tapped his clipboard. "Turnover day will be busy, so I'm putting you in charge of making sure all of my boxes sitting in port make it on board."

Millie flipped the papers and glanced at the inventory list. "How many boxes are we talking about?"

"Twenty and a large crate with a special surprise. I've already talked to Sharky down in maintenance to make sure the stevedores take special care of my deliveries."

"What's in the large crate?" Millie shifted her gaze from the paper to Andy.

"It's a surprise," Andy grinned. "You'll have to wait and see." The office phone rang.

Millie pushed her chair back as Andy reached for his phone. "Don't forget your papers."

"Right." Millie snatched the papers off the table, folded them in thirds and tucked them in her jacket pocket. She started to ask Andy where he wanted her to store his stuff, but he was already on the phone.

The rest of the afternoon flew by and later that evening, Millie hosted the *Fond Farewell* show in the main theater, followed by *Killer Karaoke* in the atrium. Her last two stops were the piano bar and the nightclub.

Before turning in, she radioed Danielle to make sure she hadn't changed her mind about camping out on the sofa bed.

Danielle assured her that although she was still upset over Tonya's unexpected death, she was exhausted from the mental stress of the days' events and all she wanted to do was sleep.

Convinced Danielle would be okay by herself, Millie headed to the apartment where she found Nic dozing in the living room recliner, the television blaring. Scout, the couple's teacup Yorkie, was curled up in his lap.

She tiptoed across the room and patted Scout's head before gently easing the remote from her husband's hand.

"Huh?" Startled, Nic's eyes flew open. "I didn't hear you come in."

"Because you were sawing logs," Millie teased. "I'm sorry I woke you."

"It's okay." Nic lifted his arms over his head and Scout hopped off his lap.

She picked him up and held him close. "My two sleepy heads are all tuckered out."

Nic slowly stood. "It was a long day. I spent part of my evening on a conference call with Dave Patterson, Donovan and the bigwigs at corporate discussing the crewmember's death."

"What a terrible situation," Millie shook her head. "We found out this morning that before her death, Tonya filed a complaint against Danielle."

"It appears Ms. Rivera's past on board the Marquise of the Seas was troubled, as well. We're still trying to figure out how she ended up on our ship instead of being put on temporary leave."

Millie perked up. "Really? I heard she filed a complaint and there was some sort of problem on board the other ship, but didn't hear any of the details."

"Oh no." Nic began shaking his head. "I'm sorry I said anything."

"Danielle is the number one suspect since she and Tonya disliked each other," Millie said. "Okay, so you can't tell me what the problem was. Will whatever it is clear Danielle's name?"

"Maybe," Nic answered vaguely. "Patterson is still investigating, that's all I can say."

Millie followed her husband up the stairs to the bedroom. "This is going to drive me crazy."

"And that's what I love about you." Nic stopped at the top of the stairs and wrapped his arms around his wife. "Even after an exhausting day of work, your mind is still racing ninety miles an hour."

He kissed her forehead and took a step back. "Tomorrow is turnover day and we have to be up early. I suggest we let it go for now and get some rest."

"But..."

"Shhh." Nic pressed a finger to Millie's lips. "I'll be out in a minute."

Millie waited until the bathroom door closed before making her way to her nightstand where she pulled out her small notepad and an ink pen.

She'd recently gotten into the habit of jotting down important notes, most often in the middle of the night when she was wide awake and suddenly remembered something important.

She flipped the top open and began scribbling, *complaint filed, Marquise of the Seas, should have been on temporary leave, empty pill bottle planted in Danielle's jacket.* Millie thought of something else. In big, bold letters, she wrote. ***Don't forget Andy's boxes.***

Nic emerged from the bathroom and he and Millie traded places. By the time she finished getting ready, Nic was in bed and fast asleep. She tiptoed to the edge of the bed and slipped under the covers.

Millie clasped her hands and prayed for Tonya's family, for Danielle and that Patterson would figure out what happened to the poor woman quickly.

Scout waited for Millie to settle in before sandwiching himself between Nic and her. The last thing she remembered hearing was her pup's soft snores before drifting off to sleep.

Exhausted, Millie slept through the night and woke with a start when the alarm clock blared.

"Is it time to get up already?" Nic groaned and rolled out of bed. "I need a vacation."

"Me too," Millie threw the covers back. "I'm getting too old for these long days and short nights."

Since Nic needed to be on the bridge early to greet the harbor pilot and begin the painstaking task of maneuvering the large ship into Biscayne Bay, he headed to the bathroom first while Millie and Scout went downstairs.

Millie began brewing a strong pot of coffee and joined her pup on the balcony. She was still standing there when Nic stuck his head out. "Thanks for the coffee. I'll see you later."

"You're welcome," Millie gave him a quick kiss and watched him walk out the front door. She wasn't far behind him in getting ready. Her first stop was Andy's office to go over the day's marching orders.

After a brief staff meeting, she made her way to the *Marseille Lounge* where the diamond and platinum guests were waiting to disembark. The disembarkation process was running right on schedule, so she strode to the theater where the self-assist guests had congregated, waiting to be among the first off.

She navigated her way through a maze of luggage to reach the crewmember in charge of the group. Today it was Alison, one of the ship's dancers. "How's it going?"

"Fine. I'm hearing only minor grumbling about the wait," Alison replied. "I think this group is setting some sort of record for the most luggage carried off in self-assist."

It always amazed Millie how much luggage passengers brought on board, and insisted on taking off themselves. All passengers were offered the option of setting their luggage in the hall outside their cabin the night before returning to the home port of Miami, where the crew would transfer it to a designated holding area.

Once the ship docked, the luggage was sorted by colored tag and placed inside the terminal where the passengers collected it after disembarking.

According to Cat, who ran the gift shop, it was a normal occurrence for frantic passengers, dressed in the ship's bathrobes, to show up at the store, looking for something to wear after setting their luggage out the night before and forgetting to keep a change of clothes with them.

"Call me if you need anything." Millie tapped the top of her radio and retraced her steps, smiling at several of the guests and wishing them safe travels.

Her next stop was the atrium, where Andy was already waiting, radio in hand and belting out orders. "The elite and self-assist passengers are raring to go. I'm waiting for Suharto to give us the all-clear, that the gangway is in place and we can start moving the masses."

It was another fifteen minutes before Suharto, the crewmember in charge of gangway security, finally gave Andy a thumbs up.

The diamond and platinum guests were the first off, followed by the self-assist. After the self-assist cleared the gangway, the rest of the passengers began making their way off the ship.

The morning passed in a blur as Millie thanked guests for cruising with them and invited them back.

It was nine o'clock before Millie checked her watch. Her feet were starting to ache and her stomach growled. "Do you mind if I grab a quick bite to eat?"

"No. Now would be the perfect time since the crowds are starting to thin," Andy said. "I'll hang out here for another half hour or so and then take my break."

"Perfect." Millie's radio began to blare. It was Sharky.

"Millie, do you copy?"

Millie lifted her radio. "Go ahead Sharky."

"I need you to meet me in the zone six loading area. We got a problem."

Chapter 4

"I hope he's not having an issue with my deliveries," Andy said. "Can you swing by there before taking your break?"

"Aye-aye, Andy." Millie lifted her hand in a mock salute and headed to the nearest stairwell. The loading zone on deck zero was several flights down. If Millie's memory served her correctly, it was directly under the atrium.

She hurried to the lower deck and maintenance area where she picked up the pace as she made her way to zone six. Up ahead, Millie spied Sharky and his scooter parked off to the side. Directly behind him were towering stacks of boxes. "What's up?"

"This." Sharky pulled an unlit cigar from his mouth and jabbed it at the boxes. "I need to move

Andy's boxes pronto. They're in my way and blocking the loading area."

"I see a clear path...clear as a bell."

"Yeah, well wait until I haul this baby on board." Sharky hopped off his scooter. "Follow me."

Millie followed him down the ramp and peered over his shoulder at a large wooden crate. "That belongs to Andy, too?"

"Yep and it's marked *fragile*. Andy told me he would have my hide if anything happened to this one."

"Do you know what it is?"

"Nope, but it's got a funny smell. Wherever you decide to put it, I would make sure it's airtight or well-ventilated."

"What kind of smell?" Millie took a tentative step toward the large crate.

"Manure, for sure. I can smell manure a mile away," Sharky said.

Millie opened her mouth to say something and promptly shut it. Maybe she didn't want to know why Sharky recognized the smell.

"Well?" Sharky eyed her expectantly. "Where do you want my guys to put the other boxes and this monstrosity?"

"To be honest, I'm open to suggestions."

"I can think of a coupla places that are secure and out of the way."

"An empty walk-in freezer?" Millie said the first thing that popped into her head.

"Are you kidding? Annette would have my hide if I hauled this smelly thing into her pristine kitchen. I was thinking more along the lines of the morgue or maybe the ship's jail."

"Ah." Millie lifted a brow. "There's plenty of room in the ship's holding cell if we store it off to the side. First, I'll need to run it by Patterson."

She promptly radioed Patterson, who didn't reply. Millie suspected he was tied up, meeting with Tonya Rivera's family. "I don't think he's going to answer my call. He's meeting with one of the crewmember's family."

"The dead chick's family? I heard she bit the dust, lying in bed and the roommate is the only suspect," Sharky said.

"She didn't do it," Millie said.

"Who?"

"Danielle Kneldon. She did not murder Tonya Rivera, her cabin mate."

"Wait a minute." Sharky sucked in a breath. "Are you telling me Tonya Rivera is the crewmember who died?"

"Yes," Millie nodded. "Danielle and I found her in her bunk."

"Well, that explains a lot."

"Explains what?"

"Her name is on a bunch of deliveries. I was waiting for her to come down here and sign for them. She's been real good about getting down here early every Saturday, as soon as the ship docks, but she never showed up this morning."

Millie's pulse ticked up a notch. "What kind of boxes?"

"Spa deliveries. You know…massage oils, creams, lotions…the stuff that costs big bucks just so you can stink. Not stink like Andy's box, but girly stink."

"Interesting."

"Tonya was also picking up boxes for that kooky needle dude, the puncturist," Sharky said.

"Acupuncturist," Millie corrected. "Are you talking about Stephen Chow?"

"Yeah. He was coming down here and signing for his own stuff. Then Tonya was signing for his deliveries, plus the spa deliveries. I guess cuz they're both in the same department."

"Do you know what was in his boxes?" Millie asked.

"Not a clue. If I had to guess, it was lots of sharp needles." Sharky made a gagging sound. "No way would I let someone stick a bunch of pins in me like a voodoo doll."

"Can I see the delivery packages?"

"Maybe." Sharky jabbed his finger at the crate. "But first, what are we gonna do with this thing?"

"I'm leaning towards putting it in the holding cell, aka the jail cell. I have the access card and code to get in, so I'll have to be there. I'm not sure how thrilled Patterson will be about me storing it there."

"Sometimes it's better to ask for forgiveness than permission," Sharky said. "At least that's my motto. What about Andy's other boxes?"

"I say we put them in his office. I think there's plenty of room," Millie said. "Before I head to the holding cell, I would like to see the boxes with Tonya's name on them."

"Sure thing." Sharky climbed the ramp and stepped inside the ship's holding area. They zigzagged past several crates before stopping abruptly in front of some smaller, white boxes. "These are the spa deliveries."

Millie knelt down for a closer inspection. Sure enough, the boxes were addressed to Siren of the Seas, Spa Department, Port of Miami, Miami, Florida, attention Tonya Rivera. "You're sure these are all spa products?"

"Yeah, I mean that's what Tonya told me. The boxes are heavy. I wouldn't try to lift them. Except for this one." Sharky nudged a small brown box with the tip of his work boot. "This one's different than the others, although it still says signature required."

"Can I open one of them, just to check it out?" Millie shifted to inspect the brown box.

"Sorry, no can do." Sharky shook his head. "Patterson called down here first thing this morning, asking a bunch of questions about deliveries, who signed, who picked up."

"What did you tell him?"

"Most are delivered to their designated areas, except for the ones needing a signature. He's coming down here to check them out."

"You said I could look at them," Millie argued.

"Looking and touching are two different things." Sharky scratched his chin, eyeing Millie thoughtfully. "I almost got in trouble last time I let you start digging through stuff."

"I would never intentionally get you in trouble," Millie said. "Please?"

"Oh…all right. But you can't open it." Sharky handed Millie the small box.

It was light. She gave it a gentle shake.

"Don't do that!" Sharky lunged forward and snatched the box from Millie. "You might be tampering with evidence."

"It never concerned you before." Millie switched tactics. "What about a return label. Does it say who shipped it?"

"Maybe." A sly smile lit Sharky's face. "You really want to take a closer look?"

"I do. One of these boxes might contain an important clue."

"Hold on a sec." Sharky tapped his foot on the floor. "It's negotiation time, Millie…You scratch my back, I scratch yours."

"What do you want?" Millie asked bluntly.

"Now that you ask…" Sharky studied the box and she could see the wheels spinning in his head. "What's Annette up to these days?"

"Oh brother. Here we go again." Millie crossed her arms. "You and Annette already went out on a date."

"You call her meeting me at my buddy's restaurant, dragging you along for a quick meal that lasted maybe twenty minutes tops and then you two took off before I could even pay the bill a date?" Sharky whined.

"It's called speed dating," Millie joked. "It's all the rage."

"It wasn't a date. If I let you snap a few pictures of Tonya's boxes, will you promise to try to negotiate another meeting?"

"You make it sound like a business venture."

Sharky ignored Millie's sarcastic reply. "Well?"

"Sure," Millie said. "Try is the key word. You know Annette. I can't promise you anything."

"You're good, Millie." Sharky clamped down on the end of his cigar. "I have complete confidence in you. I'll line the boxes up and you take the pictures."

Sharky made quick work of lining up the spa boxes. He placed the small brown box at the end. Millie followed along and snapped several pictures of the labels and boxes with her cell phone's camera. "Perfect. Thanks for helping me out, Sharky."

"My pleasure. Don't forget about our agreement."

"How could I? You won't let me." Millie nodded toward the large crate, still sitting on the dock. "When do you want me to meet your guys to drop this monstrosity off?"

"No time like the present, before Patterson catches wind of what we're doing and stops us."

"Okay." Millie frowned. "What if he makes me move it out of the holding cell?"

"That's your problem."

"That's what I thought you would say." Millie thanked Sharky again and headed to the back of the ship and up one deck to wait for the delivery. Thankfully, it was only a matter of minutes.

Millie opened the door and watched the crewmember wheel the crate inside. "Thank you."

"I'm heading back to pick up the other boxes for Andy Walker."

"Perfect. Those will be stored in the office behind the theater's stage. I'll meet you there."

She waited for the worker to leave before slowly approaching the crate. Millie leaned in and sniffed the corner. "Gross."

Sharky was right. There was a rancid odor emanating from the crate. "What in the world is that awful smell?"

Anxious to escape the noxious odor, she hurried into the hall and yanked the door shut behind her. *Wait until Patterson gets a whiff of this.*

She stopped long enough to leave Patterson a note and then hurried to the theater and Andy's office. The worker and another member of the maintenance crew, arrived moments later.

She showed them where to unload the boxes and thanked them before getting down to the business of inspecting each of them, and inventorying the items against the list Andy had given her.

There were more fall garlands, several festive cornucopias, a jack-o'-lantern and smiling witch piñata, grinning ghosts, trick or treat goodie bags and an array of cheap children's masks. The list went on and on.

It took Millie a solid hour to sort through the items, and other than a couple of damaged trinkets everything was accounted for.

She jotted Andy a note, letting him know she'd inventoried everything and that his stinky crate was stored inside the ship's holding cell.

Millie still hadn't eaten and was beginning to feel lightheaded, so she headed to the buffet where the employees were bustling back and forth, setting out large trays of food. She loaded her plate with slices of roasted turkey, crispy fried chicken, a mound of French fries and two large scoops of creamy macaroni and cheese.

On her way out, she grabbed a warm roll and balanced it on top of her plate before searching for an empty table. Brody, Danielle's boyfriend and one of the ship's security guards, was seated at a table by the window.

"Hey, Brody. Do you mind if I join you?"

"Not at all, Millie. Have a seat." Brody slid a set of silverware across the table. "I figured I better eat before the place fills up."

"It won't be long now. Who knew waiting in long lines, lugging luggage on board the ship and fighting the crowds to get through security could make people so hungry?" Millie joked.

"Right? I thought Danielle was going to meet me for lunch, but it doesn't look like she's gonna make it," Brody said.

"She's had a couple of tough days." Millie unwrapped the silverware and placed the napkin in her lap. "I was going to check on her first thing this morning, but I've been on the go since the moment my feet hit the floor."

"Danielle, too." Brody took a big bite of burger. "I stayed with her for a while last night after her shift ended. She's upset about Tonya."

Millie's heart sank. "Poor thing. I invited her to come stay with us and sleep on the sofa bed. She said she wanted to stay in her own place and assured me she would be okay."

"She didn't want to bother you." Brody hesitated and Millie could tell from the look on his face, he was about to say something.

"There's something else.""Uh-huh."

Chapter 5

"Danielle put in a request to transfer out of the entertainment department," Millie guessed.

"Nope." Brody stared at his plate.

"You can't leave me hanging," Millie said. "What is it?"

"Danielle turned in her notice the day before yesterday."

"She what? Why did she do that?" A tumble of thoughts ran through Millie's mind.

"She figured if she threatened to quit, Donovan and Andy would take her seriously and move Tonya to another cabin."

"And now Tonya's dead." Millie sawed off a piece of turkey and chewed thoughtfully.

"It was rough. Now Danielle is scared Donovan and Andy are gonna accept her resignation."

"Or that it's some sort of indication of guilt."

"Yep." Brody dropped his napkin on top of his empty plate. "I gotta get back to work. Don't repeat what I said to Danielle."

"I won't," Millie promised. "Thanks for the heads up."

"I hope she doesn't leave." Brody gave Millie a sad smile and trudged off. He stopped long enough to place his dirty dishes in the bin by the door and then disappeared from sight.

No wonder Danielle was so upset. Would Donovan and Andy accept her resignation? Sure, Danielle could be headstrong, opinionated, reckless and impulsive. She also had a heart of gold, and there wasn't anything she wouldn't do for one of her friends.

Millie gobbled up the rest of her food and dashed out of the restaurant. She needed help and although she promised Brody she wouldn't breathe a word to Danielle, she didn't promise she wouldn't tell Cat and Annette what had transpired.

The *Ocean Treasures* gift shop was closed and the lights were off. Millie caught a glimpse of movement near the back. It was Cat. She tapped lightly on the glass and her friend hurried to let her in.

"Hey, Millie. I ran into Annette a little while ago. She told me Andy has you hopping with his new fall festival schedule of events."

"No kidding. Andy is going overboard, determined to win his bet with Claudia, the cruise director on board the Baroness of the Seas."

"I know all about it." Cat waited until Millie stepped inside the store and then locked the door behind them. "He ordered a bunch of fall trinkets to sell in the store. I was just unpacking some of the boxes."

Millie followed her friend to the back. She watched as Cat reached inside a box and pulled out a keychain that resembled a scarecrow. "The eyes light up. Check it out."

Cat pressed a button to demonstrate before handing it to Millie. "Clever, huh? There are ghost ones, too. Flip it over."

Millie flipped it over. *Siren of the Seas* was etched on the back. "Cute. My grandchildren would love these. I'll have to buy a couple."

"So what's up?"

"It's Danielle. Did you hear about the death of her cabin mate?"

"Yes." Cat nodded solemnly. "I also heard the woman and Danielle detested each other and she filed a complaint."

"Patterson searched the cabin and found a prescription bottle in Danielle's work jacket. She swears up and down someone planted the bottle. I believe her."

"That's not Danielle's thing," Cat said. "Do you think the cabin mate planted it before her death?"

"Possibly," Millie admitted. "There's one more thing and you have to promise you won't breathe a word."

Cat lifted her hand. "I promise."

"I found out Danielle submitted her resignation. She was trying to force Donovan and Andy to move Tonya out of their cabin."

"Oh no." Cat wrinkled her nose. "If it's true, it would look suspicious, like Danielle may have played a part in Tonya's death. I'm sure her resignation is on hold pending the investigation."

"Good point. Remember, we're not supposed to know about it."

"My lips are sealed." Cat made a zipping motion across her lips. "What are we going to do?"

"We're going to try to figure out what happened to Tonya. I'm starting to suspect foul play somewhere along the way. Healthy young women don't die in their sleep." Millie remembered the spa deliveries with Tonya's name on them. "Sharky said Tonya was picking up deliveries for the spa department where she worked."

"That doesn't strike me as suspicious," Cat said. "I sign for store deliveries, too."

"He also said most of the deliveries were heavy boxes, full of spa products, except for one. It was light and when I shook it, it rattled, almost like it was empty or there wasn't much inside."

"Sharky wouldn't let you open it?"

"Nope, but he did let me snap a few pictures."

"For free?" Cat chuckled. "You mean he didn't charge you money or cut some sort of deal?"

"Yes." Millie sighed heavily. "We made a deal."

"Let me guess…it involves Annette."

"Of course. He claims he got ripped off on his one and only date with her, and honestly, I kind of agree. Sharky was upset when Annette insisted on meeting him at the lunch location and when he found out I was tagging along, he was crushed."

"I remember you mentioning it," Cat said. "Wasn't it like the quickest meal on record and then Annette ran out?"

"Before Sharky even had time to pay for the meal, so now he's insisting I convince Annette to go on a second date or in his words, a 'meeting.'"

"How does Annette feel about a second date?"

"She doesn't know yet. I'll have to wait for the perfect opportunity to approach her about it, when she's in the right mood."

"Which may be never," Cat joked.

"I have to admit, I admire Sharky's tenacity. He doesn't take 'no' for an answer. Maybe that's what Annette needs...persistence."

Millie pulled her cell phone from her pocket, switched it on and scrolled until she found the pictures of the boxes. "Here are the pictures." She handed her phone to Cat.

Cat slipped her reading glasses on and studied the first picture before scrolling to the next one. "These are definitely spa boxes. A few have accidentally shown up on my doorstep. Sharky is right. They're full of lotions, oils, candles, you name it."

"There are more," Millie said. "Keep going." She watched as her friend continued scrolling through the pictures.

"Ah. I found the picture of the small brown box." Cat tapped the screen to enlarge the picture. "You said this one was light and it rattled when you shook it?"

"Yep. Sharky wouldn't let me hang onto it long enough to take a closer look. Patterson was going to stop by the delivery area to check them out."

"Which is what he should do, especially if there's a chance whatever was inside might help the authorities figure out what happened to Tonya. I don't see a return label." Cat held out the phone and then snatched it back. "Wait. I think I see something else...that's what I thought."

"You found something?"

"Maybe." Cat turned the phone toward Millie.

"I see an orange label with three small letters inside. What am I looking at?"

"A drug manufacturer's logo."

Chapter 6

"Drug store drugs?" Millie blinked rapidly.

"Yep," Cat confirmed. "I was taking one of their anti-depressants until my best friends decided I needed help and hooked me up with an amazing counselor."

"And we're glad we did," Millie said. "So let me get this straight…Tonya was in charge of signing for the products going to the ship's spa. She was also signing for boxes from a drug manufacturer."

"Which would explain why the box was lighter than the others." Cat handed Millie her phone. "It sounds like she may have taken one of the empty bottles and planted it in Danielle's jacket to frame her."

"So maybe she did overdose on drugs." Millie slipped her cell phone into her pocket. "Once Patterson opens the box with Tonya's name on it, he'll realize Danielle is innocent."

"At least we hope so."

"Right. That still doesn't explain what she was doing with a box full of prescription drugs."

"Maybe she was involved in some sort of pill mill." Cat clutched her chest. "Oh my gosh. If that's true, the only person on board this ship who can write a prescription is Joe."

"Joe" was Doctor Joseph Gundervan, who was also Cat's boyfriend.

"Let's not freak out yet. It could be Tonya had a connection on the outside who was supplying her with the stuff."

"Right. Some of the ports, particularly the smaller islands, are havens for drug thugs."

"I think it's time to do a little sleuthing at the spa," Millie said. "Tomorrow won't work. It's a sea day and I'm sure Andy will have me busy working on his fall festivities."

"Monday we're in port. That would be a good day." Cat patted the counter. "I have some free time on Monday. I've been thinking of checking out the new spa services. I could go with you," she offered.

"Perfect. I'll check with Danielle. For now, I better get back to work." Millie thanked Cat for the information and told her she'd follow up later with details about the spa visit.

Millie began to hum as she strolled out of the store, certain she was one step closer to clearing Danielle's name. Now if only Andy and Donovan would reject Danielle's resignation.

She forced the troubling thought from her mind and joined Andy to greet the first wave of passengers, the diamond and platinum guests, as they ascended the gangway.

Millie chatted with several returning guests she knew by name. A steady stream of passengers continued to arrive and she fielded questions about the buffet, evening entertainment, and made a point of mentioning the fall theme, which would be in full swing.

Finally, there was a lull in the arrivals and she turned to her boss. "I inventoried all of your fall goodies. What's the next step?"

"I'm glad you asked." Andy cleared his throat and pulled a folded sheet of paper from his pants pocket. "This is a tentative revised schedule for tomorrow. I'm still working on incorporating the new activities into the rest of the week."

Millie scanned the sheet. "You are going gangbusters."

"Of course. I'm going to do everything in my power to make sure Claudia doesn't win this bet." Andy rubbed his hands together. "And you're going to help me. I'm putting you in charge of decorating starting this afternoon. Kevin volunteered to help. It shouldn't take the two of you long. Since tomorrow is a sea day, we'll have plenty of time to roll out our new fall activities."

Andy and Millie wandered to the stairwell. "Have you spoken with Danielle today?"

"No," Millie said. "Not yet. I need to track her down to see how she's doing." She didn't mention the discovery that Tonya was signing for a box from a pharmaceutical company.

She knew Andy wouldn't be happy if he thought she was nosing around in Tonya's death, not that she'd done it intentionally. Andy was the one who sent her to the loading dock to handle his deliveries.

Before she tracked Danielle down, she needed to stop by the galley to chat with Annette. Millie peeked through the galley porthole before easing the door open.

Amit, Annette's right hand man, was standing with his back to her, hunched over a large mixer.

Millie snuck up behind him. "Whatcha making?"

Amit stiffened and stumbled backwards. "Miss Millie. You scared me."

"I'm sorry. I couldn't resist." She pointed at the mixing bowl. "What are you making?"

"I'm working on another batch of pumpkin crunch cake for Miss Annette. Your boss...he give us a whole list of foods he want us to make. You must try it." Amit motioned Millie to follow him across the galley where rows of bread tins lined the gleaming stainless steel counter. "I just pulled these from the oven."

Amit carefully sliced off a generous piece of the warm cake and handed it to Millie.

"Thank you." Millie tore off a large chunk and took a big bite. The rich aroma of cinnamon wafted up. The cake nearly melted in her mouth. "This is delicious."

"I still need to add the cream cheese frosting to the top," Amit said.

"It's perfect the way it is." Millie took another bite. "My goodness. What else are you making?"

"We try making pumpkin bisque, spiced apple cider, butternut squash…so many new recipes."

"I bet Annette is ready to rip her hair out," Millie joked.

"She not happy. Mr. Andy, he better steer clear until she settle down."

"My ears are burning." Annette tromped across the galley and joined them. "Andy is driving me crazy. I told him no more recipes. If he shows up again, I'm going to put an apron on him and put him to work."

"The pumpkin crunch cake is delicious," Millie said. "I can't wait to see what else you add to the menu. Keep me in mind if you need a taste tester."

"Of course." Annette placed a fisted hand on her hip. "Heard Danielle's cabin mate died in her sleep. How's she doing?"

"Good and bad." Millie briefly explained all that had happened and ended with Brody's confession that Danielle submitted her resignation. "We can't tell anyone."

"Whew! That's terrible. I won't utter a peep," Annette promised. "I wonder if Donovan and Andy will accept it."

"I hope not. I'm going to try to talk to Danielle after I leave here."

"Sounds like Tonya was peddling prescription drugs."

"I'm beginning to think so." Millie showed Annette the pictures she'd taken of the spa boxes and the smaller pharmacy box. "Tonya's death may not have been due to natural causes. What if someone did her in?"

"Like who?"

"There was some sort of boyfriend Danielle mentioned. I think she said his name was Arvin something. There's also Tonya's boss, the spa manager, Camille. She might be able to shed some light on Tonya's activities."

"Camille must've trusted Tonya if she allowed her to sign for the spa products. You're saying Sharky told you that?"

"Yes. I was downstairs picking up Andy's half a bazillion boxes of fall goodies and we got on the subject of Tonya and the deliveries. Speaking of Sharky, I kind of owe him a favor since he let me snap pictures of Tonya's deliveries."

"What kind of favor?" Annette eyed her friend suspiciously. "I hope it doesn't involve me."

"Well…" Millie shifted uncomfortably. "He feels like he got ripped off on your lunch date. I think he's hoping you might go out with him again."

"Ripped off?" Annette roared. "I met him for lunch, we chatted, we left."

"It was one of the fastest lunches I've ever eaten," Millie argued. "You have to admit we inhaled our food, not to mention you refused to ride to the restaurant with him *and* you dragged me along."

"I'm out." Annette lifted her hands. "He needs to find a new love interest. There's zero mutual attraction between us and there never will be. Another date will give him false hope."

"Are you sure?"

"One hundred percent. You know what?" Annette untied her apron and tossed it on the counter. "I'm going down there right now and nip this thing in the bud."

"You should be flattered." Millie followed her friend to the galley door.

"I was and it lasted about five seconds." Annette stepped into the hall. "He's wasting his time. There's nil chance of a spark developing between us. The quicker I point that out, the faster Sharky's heartbreak will heal."

"Be nice." Millie hurried after her friend.

"I will. My plan is to suggest bargaining with food again, and forget about the dates. I think that's a fair substitute."

When they reached deck zero, Annette paused. "Right or left?"

"Sharky's office is to the right. To the left is the loading dock. I'm sure the ship's crewmembers are working their tails off, trying to get everything on board before we set sail."

"Which means Sharky is probably sitting in his office with his feet up on the desk, chomping on the end of his unlit cigar."

"What kind of boss would hide out in his office while the people under him are busting their butts?" Millie asked.

"Sharky." Annette stopped in front of the maintenance office. From the hall, the women could see the office lights were on. "Eh? I rest my case." She gave it a couple of quick raps before pushing the door open.

Millie discovered Annette was partially right. Sharky was in his office, seated at his desk with a clipboard in front of him. He looked up and then did a double take. "Hello, ladies."

"Hey, Sharky," Millie said. "We're sorry to bother you."

"No bother. I was going over the cargo manifests. How can I help you two lovely ladies?"

"I talked to Annette about your…earlier request." Millie swallowed nervously. "She decided to come down here and speak with you face-to-face."

"What request?" Sharky asked.

"The one you made earlier, when you asked me to try to negotiate another meeting, I mean, date with Annette," Millie said.

"I did?" Sharky shook his head. "You must be confusing me with someone else, cuz I don't remember any such thing."

"Sharky Kiveski, you certainly did." Millie pointed at Sharky. "You told me I couldn't take pictures of the spa packages unless I promised to talk to Annette."

"I said that?" Sharky tapped his pen on top of the clipboard, appearing genuinely confused by Millie's statement. "Are you sure? I don't recall making the request. Even if I did, I rescind it. Annette and me…we're just not made for each other."

"Perfect," Annette beamed. "Have a great day."

Millie scowled at Sharky. "I know what you said."

"Meh. Does it matter now?" Sharky asked.

"I gotta get going. See you later." Annette gave Millie a light punch in the arm and began humming as she exited the office.

Millie waited until the door closed behind her friend before turning her attention to Sharky. "What was that all about?"

"It's called reverse psychology. I've been doing a little research. Annette is a tough cookie, but I got her number." Sharky tapped the side of his forehead. "Just wait. Before long, she'll be eatin' out of my hand."

"You want her to think you're not interested, so she'll start pursuing you? Now, that, I have to see." Millie reached for the doorknob before turning back. "While I'm here, I was wondering...did Patterson stop by to check out the boxes with Tonya's name on them?"

"Oh yeah." Sharky straightened his back. "He had my guys load them, along with the other smaller box, on a hand cart and then he took off."

"He didn't open any of the boxes?"

"Nope. I was hoping he would cuz I'm kinda curious about what was inside the smaller box. Patterson inspected the outsides, made a comment about paying a visit to the medical center and then left."

Chapter 7

"Interesting," Millie murmured. "I believe I'm developing a slight migraine and it's time for me to stop by the medical center myself."

After leaving Sharky's office, Millie decided to postpone her visit to the ship's medical center for two reasons. It was time for her to get ready for the mandatory safety drill and she didn't want to chance running into Patterson.

Millie joined her safety group in the theater's deck three stairwell where she donned her bright yellow safety jacket. She stood near the entrance and scanned the guests' keycards to make sure everyone in her safety zone showed up to attend the mandatory drill.

There were a few minor grumbles, mostly from previous guests who complained they'd attended the drill numerous times and didn't see the point. She smiled politely and motioned for them to join the others inside the theater.

As soon as the final emergency alarm sounded, announcing the drill was under way, Nic's solemn voice echoed overhead as he explained the purpose of the safety drill and the signal.

Several of the crewmembers and staff demonstrated how to wear the life vests. They pointed out the safety features and – Millie's favorite part – how to blow the whistle.

The safety demonstration ended and the crowds made their way out of the theater. Millie spotted Danielle near the front, talking to some of the other staff.

Millie wandered down the center aisle to join Danielle, who looked a little pale. "Are you feeling all right?"

"I'm fine." Danielle flipped her bangs out of her eyes. "Patterson showed up at my cabin bright and early this morning to search it again. I think he's onto something. When I tried to ask him about the investigation he cut me off, claiming he was still gathering information."

"I found out a few things myself," Millie said.

"You started your own investigation?"

"Yes, but not intentionally. I was downstairs collecting some of Andy's goodies for his fall festivities. While Sharky and I were talking, I discovered Tonya was signing for deliveries."

"I knew that. Tonya told me it was part of her job," Danielle said. "Her boss, Camille, put her in charge of unpacking and inventorying spa products."

"That wasn't all." Millie glanced around and lowered her voice. "There was another box on the dock with Tonya's name on it. It was from a large pharmaceutical company. Check it out."

Millie pulled her cell phone from her pocket, switched it on and then handed it to Danielle. "Sharky let me take pictures of the boxes including the smaller one. At first glance, it looks as if the box is unmarked, but Cat's eagle eye noticed a small logo in the corner. It's a pharmaceutical logo."

"No kidding?" Danielle studied the screen. "Tonya was handling prescription drugs? I'm sure the spa isn't allowed to dispense prescription drugs."

"They can't, which is why when Patterson picked up the boxes, he mentioned to Sharky that he was going to pay a visit to the medical center."

Danielle handed the phone back. "He thinks Doctor Gundervan was involved?"

"I'm not sure. What I do know, is that questioning Gundervan would be the most logical place to start, which is why I plan on paying a visit to the medical center later."

"Can I go with you?" Danielle asked.

"It will look suspicious if we go together, not to mention you were Tonya's cabin mate and if

Patterson confronted Gundervan about Tonya's delivery, he'll get suspicious."

"True." Danielle snapped her fingers. "I've got it. We could head up to the spa under the guise of me pulling a muscle in my back and see if an employee offers me some drugs."

"That sounds like a great plan. First, I feel a migraine coming on and it's time to head to the medical clinic."

Danielle trailed behind Millie. "Did you get all of Andy's deliveries squared away?"

"Oh yeah. He bought so much junk…er…stuff for this fall blowout; I had a hard time figuring out where to put it. I know for sure decorating is on my schedule."

"Here's mine." Danielle pulled a sheet of paper from her pocket and handed it to Millie. "He wasn't kidding about assigning me to the kiddo's activities. I'm in charge of pumpkin painting, costume making, he's even managed to find a way to create a makeshift hayride using an old prop he found stored in the bowels of the ship."

"Really?" Millie studied the list. "The haunted dining room mystery dinner sounds intriguing."

"It's all yours," Danielle said. "I'm going to be up to my eyeballs in popcorn balls and caramel apple decorating."

"Caramel apples sound yummy." Millie handed the sheet back and glanced at her watch. "I better head to the medical center. First, I need to make sure Patterson got my note. I stored one of Andy's deliveries, a large crate, in the holding cell."

"What is it?"

"I have no idea, but it stinks…literally." Millie made a gagging sound. "Patterson will no doubt force Andy to move it."

"This, I gotta see. Is there time for me to check it out?"

"Sure. It's pretty much on my way."

The women descended the stairs to deck two where both the medical center and security office, along with the holding cell, were located.

Danielle waited for Millie to scan her keycard and punch in the special code to unlock the door. "One of these days I'm going to enjoy all of the perks you get."

"It's not all it's cracked up to be. Besides, with more privileges comes more responsibility." Millie pushed the door open and stepped inside.

The putrid smell emanating from the mysterious crate filled the small space.

"Gross." Danielle clamped her hand over her mouth.

"The smell is even worse now." Millie blinked. "It's burning my eyes."

"And my nostrils. There's a hole near the bottom." Danielle dropped to her knees and shined her cell phone's flashlight inside the hole. "It looks like it's full of packing peanuts. We need something to pry the box open."

Millie's eyes darted around the room. "We can see if Patterson has something to pry it open."

The women exited the cell/holding area and stepped into the hall. Millie made sure the door was shut before they strolled to the security office. The lights were on and when Millie knocked, there was a muffled response, so she opened the door and stuck her head inside.

Patterson was seated at his desk. "Hey, Millie."

"Hey, Patterson. I hate to bother you. I thought I should let you know I stored one of Andy's deliveries inside the holding cell. I left a message on your desk earlier when I dropped it off."

"You did?" Patterson patted his desk. "I didn't find a note. Maybe one of the other guys picked it up. Why the holding cell? Why not take it to Andy's office?"

"Because the crate stinks, literally. Danielle and I want to pry it open to see what's inside. Andy said it was a surprise, but that smell. Yuck."

"I'll give you a hand." Patterson opened one of his desk drawers and pulled out a hammer.

"You keep a hammer in your desk?" Millie chuckled. "So you can beat your staff into submission?"

"Very funny. I borrowed it from maintenance a couple of days ago and haven't had a chance to return it."

"How is it going with Tonya's investigation?" Millie couldn't help but ask.

"Captain Armati, Donovan and I met with Tonya's family this morning. As you can imagine, they're devastated by her death and are already in contact with the authorities about the investigation. Unfortunately, I couldn't tell them much."

Millie almost mentioned the deliveries and the box of pharmaceutical drugs, but decided to keep quiet. "I'm sure you sent the prescription bottle you found in Danielle's work jacket to the lab for fingerprinting."

"Yes, and at this point I believe it's a formality, Danielle. Although you know I can't share my findings, it appears that some of Ms. Rivera's on board activities are of concern."

"Like what?" Danielle asked. "I've been racking my brain trying to piece together clues of what may have happened. To be blunt, we didn't like each other. We kept conversations to a minimum. I have no idea what she did in her free time and vice versa."

"Camille, Tonya's boss, wasn't able to shed much light on Tonya's after work activities. She wasn't particularly close to her spa co-workers, but then she hasn't been on board our ship for very long. I have a call in to her previous supervisor and cabin mate on board the Marquise of the Seas to ask some questions."

"Don't forget about her employee records," Millie said.

"Who's running this investigation?" Patterson asked.

"You," Millie mumbled. "I'm just trying to help."

"I know," Patterson said. "And I appreciate the fact you want to help your friend, but I'm confident this investigation will be wrapped up soon."

Millie wondered if Patterson believed Tonya died of an accidental overdose and once the autopsy was finished, he could clear Danielle's name and close the investigation.

If Tonya was peddling prescription drugs, there were others involved. Then there was the matter of money...if Tonya was selling drugs to crewmembers or, heaven forbid, ship's passengers who visited the spa, where was the money?

Patterson interrupted her musings. "Danielle, you mentioned a crewmember by the name of

Arvin. I tracked him down and plan to meet with him this afternoon to see what he knows."

"Arvin?" Millie perked up. "What department does he work in?"

Patterson narrowed his eyes. "Why do you want to know?"

"I'm merely curious. Just because Danielle is one of my closest friends doesn't mean I'm going to stick my nose in where it doesn't belong."

"You said it – not me."

When they reached the holding cell, Patterson fished his keycard out of his pocket and scanned it before punching in the access code and stepping inside.

Millie hovered in the doorway. The same awful smell filled the small space. If possible, it smelled even worse. "Disgusting."

"What in the world?" Patterson made his way over to the large crate. After a quick examination, he wedged the hammer's claw between the lid and the frame and began prying it open.

Crack. With a quick couple of jerks and a loud splintering sound, the lid gave way. A cascade of packing peanuts poured out of the box and onto the floor.

Millie caught a glimpse of something gray and let out a yelp before bolting from the room.

Chapter 8

"It's a dead rat," Danielle gasped.

The poor, emaciated critter appeared to have been inside the box for some time.

Patterson ripped the rest of the cover off. More peanuts poured out, along with a ball of baby rats.

"Ew," Danielle cringed.

"Andy ordered a bunch of dead rats?" Patterson joked.

"No. I think he ordered the scarecrows and the rodents were a bonus." Millie pointed at two large, smiling scarecrows tucked in the back of the box.

Danielle took a tentative step forward. "I hope he didn't pay a lot of money. There's no way you're going to get me to touch those things."

"Me either." Millie took a step back.

"Mystery solved." Patterson placed a call to the maintenance department, requesting a handcart and some disinfecting supplies be brought to the holding cell.

"At least one of the mysteries is solved," Millie said. "I'll let Andy know his big surprise is a big bust."

"I need to head back upstairs." Danielle gave Millie a quick look.

"Yes. Uh…" Millie pressed the palm of her hand to her forehead. "I'm worried the awful smell is going to give me a splitting headache. I think I'll stop by the medical center for some aspirin just in case."

Danielle and Millie stepped into the hall while Patterson waited for the maintenance crew to show up and remove the offensive scarecrows, the critters and the crate.

"I'll meet up with you later," Millie said under her breath.

"Thanks, Millie."

When Millie reached the medical center, Doctor Gundervan wasn't around. Rachel Quaid, the ship's nurse was there, her back to the door as she crouched in front of the supply cabinet.

Millie cleared her throat to announce her presence.

Rachel bolted upright, banging her forehead on the cabinet door. "Ouch."

"I'm sorry, Rachel. I didn't mean to scare you." Millie briefly explained she felt a headache coming on and asked her for a packet of aspirin.

Rachel gave her an odd look. "You don't have aspirin in your apartment?"

"I do, but I'm kind of…it was a lot closer for me to pop in here and grab a pack since I was in the neighborhood and I've got to get back to work." Rachel gave her another funny look. "Okay. We store them in the back."

Millie followed her into the examining room. "I've always wondered how many passengers and crew you treat on a daily or weekly basis."

"It depends." Rachel unlocked one of the cabinets and reached inside. "During rough sea days we get a lot more patients. We also get a bunch on port days with the usual complaints…sunburns, heatstroke, pulled muscles, gastrointestinal problems from people who eat spicy foods they're not accustomed to."

"I see, but probably more crewmembers than passengers," Millie suggested.

"Not necessarily." Rachel handed Millie a packet of aspirin and shut the cabinet door.

"Do you ever run out of stuff, say for example prescription drugs and then have to purchase them in port?"

"Rarely. Joe, I mean Doctor Gundervan, doesn't like to do that. He is very particular about his prescription inventory." Rachel frowned. "You seem awfully curious about the medical center. Did Dave Patterson send you down here?"

Millie's eyes widened innocently. "No. I…I was just making conversation." She dropped the packet in her pocket. "Why would Patterson send me down here?"

"I don't know." Millie could tell from the look on Rachel's face she didn't believe her. "Do you need anything else?"

"No. I think this will do me." She thanked Rachel for the aspirin and made her way out of the medical center.

It was time to get back to work. Millie darted from event-to-event, making sure everything was running smoothly. She fleetingly wondered what Andy thought when he found out his special "surprise" harbored some surprises of its own.

While she worked, she also wondered about Tonya. If Tonya had been smuggling prescription drugs on board, how was she getting them? Surely,

Patterson would be able to pinpoint how Tonya was able to get the boxes delivered to her at the port.

But where was she storing them? A cold chill ran down Millie's spine. What if she was storing them inside her cabin and the boxes were still there, hidden so well that even Patterson couldn't find them?

During her afternoon break, she radioed Danielle to set up a time to meet. Since both women were working similar schedules, they agreed to meet at eleven o'clock outside Danielle's cabin.

The long day finally ended and Millie trudged below deck to Danielle's cabin. She was already there waiting. "Well? Did you find anything out from visiting the medical center?"

"Nope. It was a bust. Gundervan wasn't there. Rachel started to get suspicious when I asked questions about the center and how many people visited it. Yada, yada. I did think of something else."

"What?"

"Let's go inside and I'll tell you."

"Sure." Danielle waited for Millie to step inside and then closed the door behind her. "What did you think of?"

"The box of prescription drugs Tonya was going to sign for. Let's say Tonya was still here…she had to store them somewhere."

Danielle's eyes grew wide. "And if she was selling them to either crewmembers or passengers, where's the cash?"

"Bingo. Now you're thinking." Millie shifted her gaze and looked around the cabin. "I know Patterson already searched the place, but how thoroughly did he search?"

"I have no idea. I say we tear this place apart," Danielle said.

"I was hoping you would say that. You start out here and I'll start in the closets." Millie headed to the closet where she systematically removed each item.

After removing everything, she pressed her hands against the walls, the floor and the ceiling, searching for a secret compartment or panel.

The closet was clean. She carefully replaced all of the items and opened the other closet door. "This other closet is empty."

"That was Tonya's closet." Danielle gave Millie a quick glance. "The security guys were in here first thing this morning, packing her stuff up to return it to the family."

"That's a bummer." Millie began tapping the sides of the closet. "We might be wasting our time."

"Not necessarily. If Tonya was clever, she would never store the drugs or cash in her closet."

"True, you have a point." Millie closed the closet door. "I guess I'll check the bathroom."

Millie flipped the light switch on and stepped inside. "Top to bottom," she muttered as she climbed on top of the toilet seat and began pressing on the ceiling panels. She moved on to the medicine cabinet before unscrewing the showerhead.

She dug through the bathroom trash before disassembling the hairdryer.

Disappointed and coming up empty handed, she returned to the main cabin area. "I didn't find anything. How about you?"

"Nothing." Danielle wiggled the mini fridge back in place and closed the door. "If she was hiding something, it wasn't in here. I'm not ready to give up. I think we still need to visit the spa."

Millie stifled a yawn. "How about tomorrow?"

"Tomorrow is a sea day. Andy has me booked solid. I don't have any time off until Monday when we're in St. Martin," Danielle said.

"Uh-oh." Millie patted her jacket pockets. "I forgot to pick up my schedules from Andy. I'm surprised he hasn't been blowing up my radio."

"He's too busy trying to figure out how to salvage his stinky scarecrows."

"True," Millie laughed. "We should've hung around. I would've loved to see the look on his face when he saw what else was in the crate."

The women agreed to plan a spa visit on Monday, while the ship was in St. Martin.

After leaving Danielle, Millie made a mental note to try to do a little online research into Arvin's background. She would have to wait until Nic was working to log onto the home computer.

Andy's office was empty and Millie found her schedule tacked to the bulletin board.

When she reached the bridge, she found Nic, along with Second Officer Myron Greaves, on the bridge. Nic gave his wife a quick nod. "I'll be finished in half an hour or so."

"Perfect." Millie gave him a thumbs up and strolled to the apartment where Scout was waiting at the door.

She scooped him up and carried him down the hall. "Poor fella. You've been cooped up in this apartment all day."

They wandered out onto the balcony and Millie watched as he trotted over to his potty pad. "How would you like to help me tomorrow? We'll start early; maybe even sneak in a quick visit to the *Ocean Oasis*, your favorite play area up on deck."

Scout finished his business and scampered across the balcony.

"So it's a promise, we're going to hang out tomorrow."

With Nic on the bridge, Millie decided it was the perfect time to do a little snooping. She waited for the computer to fire up, and after taking a quick look at her emails, she logged onto the ship's employee information.

With a couple of clicks, she successfully pulled up the staff and crew roster and began searching for

Arvin. Thankfully, there was only one employee named Arvin. "Arvin Kurtz."

She clicked on his name and began scrolling through the screen. It was the usual employee information...date of birth, address, emergency contact information. Nothing struck her as odd or unusual.

She clicked on the second page, which listed Arvin's past work history. Millie slipped her reading glasses on and scanned the list. He was currently working his second contract with Majestic Cruise Lines.

It was the next line that got her attention. Millie's heart skipped a beat when she noticed Arvin and Tonya had something in common.

Chapter 9

Both Arvin and Tonya previously worked on board the Marquise of the Seas. Arvin was the first to transfer to the Siren of the Seas and had been working on board the ship for several months.

Millie leaned back in her chair. It wasn't uncommon for crewmembers who worked together to eventually end up on another ship together. What struck Millie as odd was the fact that they were friends.

Had Tonya and Arvin also been close on board the Marquise of the Seas?

Millie scrolled to the top, where it listed Arvin's position. He worked in the ship's recycling and waste management department, which meant the couple either met in one of the employee common areas or knew each other previously.

Unfortunately, Millie didn't know anyone who worked in the recycling department that she could question about Arvin.

The doorknob rattled and Millie frantically tapped the computer keys to exit the employee portal.

Scout hopped off Millie's lap and ran to the door to greet Nic, who picked him up and carried him back into the living room. "I figured you would be asleep by now."

"Nah. I'm trying to unwind. I guess I should be in bed since Andy is rolling out his new fall festivities tomorrow and it's going to be a busy day." Millie lifted her hands over her head to stretch. "How 'bout you? What does your schedule look like?"

"It's a sea day. I'll have some extra free time. I was wondering if you would be interested in a date night tomorrow night. We can sneak up to *The Vine* for dinner."

"I would love to have a dinner date." Nic and Millie had planned to check out the newly revamped Italian restaurant, but so far hadn't had a chance. "I'll make reservations tomorrow. What time?"

The couple discussed the reservation as they drifted out onto the balcony. The night skies were clear and the stars dazzled brightly overhead.

Millie loved to step outside on clear nights, when the ship was far from shore. It was a completely different world, and she could only envision how majestic heaven was if this was a small glimpse of God's magnificent creation.

She snuggled close to Nic as a gentle breeze lifted the tips of her hair. "Isn't this beautiful?"

"It is," Nic agreed. "Sometimes we forget how fortunate we are to see such awesome sights, which reminds me, I spoke with Ted Danvers on the phone earlier today. It appears that the Siren of the Seas will be repositioning in the spring."

Millie stiffened. "For good? Where? Will I have time to go home to say good-bye to my children?"

Nic squeezed Millie's arm. "Hold on. There's no need to panic. It's only for a season. I'm sure you'll have plenty of time to see the children before we leave."

"Only for a season?" Millie pressed a hand to her chest. "That's a relief. Where?"

"The British Isles."

"Aren't cruise ships booked months in advance?" Millie asked. "I mean, how can a cruise line move a ship on such short notice?"

"It's not. I know you don't track the ship's bookings, but the Siren of the Seas' Caribbean itinerary was dropped in April. We sail across the Atlantic to Southampton and begin our longer cruises around the Isles in early May."

"Longer cruises?"

Nic explained the itinerary would be twelve-day cruises, with more port stops and longer port days. "It should be exciting. We'll have time to explore each of the ports during the season. That was part of the deal I made with Danvers, you and I would be able to carve out some free time to see the sights."

"What if no one wants to book the Siren of the Seas and cruise the British Isles?" Millie asked.

"They have and they will. The cruises are filling up fast."

"Can I check it out online? Why didn't Andy tell me?"

"Because he couldn't." Nic led his wife back inside. They waited for Scout to join them and then Nic closed the balcony door. "You can get the full itinerary from Andy tomorrow. The excursion desk already has a copy of the excursions. You should get a copy, so you can start planning our adventures."

After the couple finished their nightly prayers, Millie lay there wide-awake for a long time. She'd never considered the ship moving across the ocean. Would she get seasick during the long voyage?

Would Nic and she actually have enough free time to explore the ports? Would she hate being thousands of miles away from home and everything she knew and loved?

As she dozed off, she asked God to give her peace. The decision was out of her hands. Finally, she fell into a fitful sleep.

*****

Millie's first thought when the alarm went off the next morning was to wonder what Andy had done with the stinky scarecrows.

Her second thought was about Danielle. Since Andy had penciled in a brief meeting with all of the entertainment staff first thing that morning, Millie made a mad dash for the closet and clean work clothes while Nic made his way into the master bathroom to get ready.

She started a pot of coffee, let Scout out for his morning break and then darted into the downstairs bathroom to get ready. Millie was once again grateful for the extra bathroom. It gave them ample elbow room to get ready at the same time.

Nic breezed into the kitchen where his wife was expertly twisting her hair into a knot. "Maybe I should cut this mess off," Millie grumbled. "I spend most of my time pulling it out of my face anyways."

"I love your long, luscious locks. I love to run my fingers through them," Nic joked.

"When's the last time you did that?"

"I don't know, but how about after our date night tonight?"

"Now that's an offer I can't resist." Millie leaned in for a long kiss while Scout trampled on top of her shoe.

"Scout agrees." Nic reached for a coffee cup.

"I promised Scout he could be my sidekick today. During our break, we're going to stop by his *Ocean Oasis* for a quick dip in the pool."

"I'm sure he'll like that." Nic glanced at his watch. "I'm off to start my day. Don't worry about breakfast. I'll order breakfast delivery once I settle in."

"It's a little early to think about food." Millie gave her husband another kiss and watched him leave before swallowing the last of her coffee. She led the pup outside for another potty break and then they strode onto the bridge.

With a quick wave to Nic and another of the ship's officers, they trekked down to Andy's office. Several members of the entertainment staff were already there, munching on donuts and sipping coffee.

Millie spied Danielle and made her way to the other side of the room. "How was last night?"

"Rough," Danielle said. "I didn't get much sleep. I spent half the night trying to figure out where Tonya might have stashed the drugs or cash, and then I wondered if we're way off."

"Attention everyone!" Andy clapped his hands. "I'll keep this meeting brief. The main reason you're all here is to make sure you have a copy of this week's revised entertainment activities. As I mentioned during my last meeting, this one is all about fall." He briefly highlighted some of the event changes before droning on about how important it was for the passengers to provide positive feedback to corporate.

He wrapped up his speech, answered a few questions and then dismissed everyone, but not before repeating how important it was to stick to the fall theme.

Millie waited until her co-workers filed out, leaving only Andy, Danielle and her in the room.

"Do you need something?" Andy asked.

"No. We were just curious...what happened to the stinky scarecrows that were in the holding cell?"

"They're downstairs being fumigated," Andy said. "I'm thinking about putting them outside the theater. Did I tell you I dug out some old Halloween flicks? We're hosting a movie marathon right here tomorrow afternoon while we're in St. Martin."

"I'm not surprised," Millie murmured.

Andy ignored the comment. "My plans include opening a popcorn stand and offering free popcorn and sodas to anyone who stops by. Millie, I'm putting you in charge of it."

"You are?" Millie fumbled with her schedule. "I...haven't had a chance to check out tomorrow's schedule. Do I have to watch horror movies?"

"Not horror movies – Halloween movies," Andy corrected. "We'll start with *It's the Great Pumpkin, Charlie Brown,* followed by *Casper the Friendly Ghost* and a couple more for the youngsters. After that, we'll start showing Halloween classics like scary *Halloween* movies."

Andy continued. "You won't have to sit through the movie marathon. I want you to be there to hand out the movie schedules, along with some sodas and popcorn and then you can leave. Other than that, just stop by every couple of hours to make sure everything is running smoothly."

"Oh…one more thing." Andy hurried to his cabinet, opened the bottom drawer and pulled out two large bags. He handed one to Millie and the other to Danielle.

"What's this?" Danielle took the bag.

"Costumes. No fall theme, weeks before Halloween, would be complete without costumes. This is part of your surprise."

"What kind of costumes?" Millie started shaking her head as she pulled out a pointed black hat with an orange band circling the rim. "Are you trying to tell me something?"

"At least you won't be dressed like a clown." Danielle held up a bright red wig.

"I even picked one out for Scout," Andy beamed. "It's in your bag, Millie."

She sifted through the bag and pulled out a miniature hot dog.

"Hot dog...get it?"

"Now that's super cute," Danielle said. "The others? Not so much."

Millie knelt on the floor to let Scout inspect his costume. He gave it a tentative sniff and then backed away. "I don't think he likes it."

"So what are you going to be dressed as, Andy?" Danielle asked.

"A cruise director."

"What if I refuse?" Millie asked bluntly.

Andy's face fell. "It's all in good fun, Millie. I want to win this contest and I'm almost positive Claudia wouldn't think to dress up." Andy hurried on. "It's not all of the time, just for the trick or treating event, the haunted house and during the movie marathon."

"Fine. I won't be a party pooper." Millie dropped Scout's hot dog costume back in the bag. "Let it be known you owe me one."

"You owe both of us," Danielle said.

"I knew you would see things my way. That's all I have for now." In Andy's mind, the subject was closed.

"I better head out for the spooky stride up on the jogging track." Millie and Danielle started for the door.

"Danielle, before you go, I would like a word with you in private," Andy said.

Danielle and Millie exchanged a quick glance.

"See you later." Millie pulled the door shut behind her and wondered if Andy wanted to discuss Danielle's resignation.

She hoped her friend had asked to withdraw her resignation, and Donovan and Andy agreed. It would be heartbreaking to have her young friend quit over a cabin mate who was no longer around.

When Millie reached the jogging track, Scout and she waited off to the side as the participants began arriving. She opened the envelope Andy had given her, labeled *Spooky Stride,* and pulled out a stack of smiling jack-o-lantern stickers.

"Those are neat." One of the guests, dressed in jogging shorts, a t-shirt and sneakers leaned over Millie's shoulder.

"I guess this is your reward for participating." Millie handed a sticker to the woman, who promptly peeled the paper off and pressed the sticker on her t-shirt.

More participants gathered around to collect a sticker before oohing and aahing over Scout, who was lapping up the lavish attention.

At seven forty-five, Scout and Millie began the trek around the jogging track. One lap in, Scout started to slow, so she picked him up and carried him.

Scout wiggled in her arms until he was peering over Millie's shoulder, watching the other walkers follow behind them.

They walked several laps, until the striders completed a mile. "That's a mile, folks." She stepped off the track, thanked them for joining her and Scout. Some of them kept going, while others stopped to say good-bye to Scout.

With the first event of the day under their belt, Millie and Scout trudged downstairs to the buffet to grab a bite to eat and something to drink.

One of the workers assembled a small bag of food for Scout while Millie loaded her plate with eggs benedict, some slices of bacon and mixed fruit. She balanced her plate, along with a cup of coffee, as they carefully made their way to Scout's *Ocean Oasis*.

When they reached the private retreat, Scout devoured his food and then frolicked in his miniature swimming pool while Millie ate.

Scout made several trips from the pool to Millie's chair to check out what she was eating. He drank some of his pool water and after tiring of his swim, he shook himself off before curling up on top of his pool towel.

They stayed as long as Millie dared. "Let me empty your pool." She drained the pool and gathered their things. With a quick stop to drop off their dirty dishes, Scout and she headed downstairs to the trivia area outside the casino bar.

Millie unlocked the storage cabinet and pulled out the pads of paper and pens. She flipped through her packet of materials, searching for the trivia questions and wasn't surprised to see that Andy had switched those out, too.

"I guess we're doing a fall trivia contest," she told Scout.

The trivia contests were one of the more popular sea day events, and Millie grudgingly admitted not only did she have a lot of fun; she learned a few things, too.

The winning trivia team received a complimentary pumpkin cream cheese muffin from the gourmet coffee bar and a gingerbread latte, the specialty drink of the month, Millie suspected was Andy's creation.

Next, it was off to check in on the St. Martin port talk being held in the *Marseille Lounge*, followed by games up on the lido deck.

Millie could see Scout was starting to tire. "Are you ready to go home?" When they reached the apartment, she nudged Scout outside for a quick trip to his potty pad.

Afterwards, Scout promptly plopped down on his doggie bed.

"You poor thing. I tuckered you out." Millie tucked several of Scout's favorite stuffed animals around him before exiting the apartment.

Captain Vitale was on the bridge with another crewmember. Nic was nowhere in sight.

Millie consulted her schedule and noticed her next event was hosting the bridge games in the library.

She made it as far as the hall when her cell phone vibrated. No one ever called her cell phone, except in the event of an emergency. "Now what?"

Chapter 10

It was a text message from Danielle, telling her she needed to talk to her ASAP.

Millie quickly texted back. *Where? I can meet you now.*

In the employee lounge.

I'm on my way. Millie shoved her phone into her pocket and darted down the stairs, taking them two at a time. Could it be Andy and Donovan accepted Danielle's resignation and she wanted to tell Millie in person that she was leaving, before word spread around the ship?

Millie always admired her young friend's upbeat personality, her determination. Yes, Danielle was a bit impulsive and there were times it got her into a little hot water.

Not that Millie had room to talk. Still, she never pegged her young friend as a quitter and that's exactly how Millie viewed Danielle's resignation.

By the time she reached the employee lounge, she was determined to talk Danielle out of leaving, or at the very least, delaying it until she had time to think about what she was doing.

She found Danielle alone inside the lounge, leaning over the pool table, pool stick in hand. "I didn't know you liked playing pool."

"That's because you never come down here." Danielle squeezed one eye shut as she pulled back the pool stick and took a shot at the cue ball. It struck another ball with a sharp *ting*. The target ball neatly dropped into a corner pocket.

"Nice. Maybe you'll teach me how to play one day." Millie changed the subject. "Is everything okay? Your message sounded urgent."

"My day was going good until I stopped by my place to swap out my walkie-talkie batteries and found my door ajar." Danielle pulled a sheet of paper from her back pocket and handed it to Millie. "I found this on the floor."

Millie unfolded the paper. *You're next.*

"You're next." She read the words aloud.

"Someone was inside my cabin. I think whoever it was is looking for something."

"We searched the place last night. It's clean."

"It *was* clean," Danielle pointed out. "There are very few people who have special keycards that are able to access crew cabins."

"You're right." Millie handed the note back. "We can get to the bottom of this real fast." She marched across the room to the wall phone. "All we have to do is ask Patterson to check the access log."

Danielle flew across the room and snatched the receiver out of Millie's hand. "No! I don't want Patterson or anyone else to know about this."

"Why not? Someone is threatening your life *and* they have access to your cabin."

"It's a long story." Danielle placed the receiver back on the hook. "I submitted my resignation before Tonya died, hoping it would force Andy and Donovan's hand and they would move Tonya out of my cabin."

"You're quitting?" Millie feigned surprise. "I never pegged you for a quitter."

"No. I mean, no I didn't plan on quitting. After Tonya died, I asked them to withdraw my resignation. Donovan said it was too late. Someone accidentally forwarded it to corporate. It's out of Andy and Donovan's hands."

Danielle explained both Andy and Donovan asked corporate to disregard the resignation, that it was sent by mistake, but after discovering Danielle's cabin mate passed away under suspicious circumstances, the management department unanimously decided to wait until hearing the outcome of Tonya's investigation to make their decision.

"So depending on how Tonya's investigation goes, I may or may not have a job, which may be the least of my worries."

"Based on everything we know, I think she overdosed," Millie said. "Patterson has the prescription delivery with Tonya's name on it. What more would the investigators need? If they determine she died of a drug overdose, I'm sure her death will be ruled accidental."

"I agree, but now there's someone on board is sneaking into my cabin and leaving threatening notes. 'I'm next' means…Tonya didn't die of an accidental overdose. Someone murdered her."

Danielle clasped her hands. "Please don't tell Patterson. He'll probably think I wrote the note. I called you because you have access to the keycard logs and can find out who was inside my cabin."

"I can, but this is serious. We need to tell Patterson," Millie said.

"I agree it's serious. Before we do that and heap more suspicion on my head, can we please take a look at the logs first?"

Millie studied Danielle's face before grudgingly agreeing. "Fine. I'll make you a deal. We'll find out whose keycard was used to get into your cabin and depending on who it was, we're going to turn them in, pronto."

"Okay. Can we go now?"

"Yes." Millie glanced at her watch. "What does your schedule look like?"

"I'm co-hosting a rumba class in twenty-five minutes. I already talked to Kevin, the instructor, and told him I had an emergency and might be late."

"Let's get a move on. We'll have to use the apartment computer."

The women stepped onto the bridge, passing by the same officers who had been there when Millie left a short time ago. Captain Vitale gave Millie a strange look, but didn't say anything.

Scout, who was still napping on his bed, barely stirred.

"Grab us an iced tea in the fridge while I turn the computer on."

Millie quickly logged into the ship's restricted access area. The keycard tracking system worked on a timing system, as well as a deck locator.

She typed in deck one, to pull up the deck access records for the day and shifted in her chair. "What time do you think they broke in?"

"I left first thing this morning and didn't return until a short time ago, which leaves all morning wide open." Danielle handed Millie a glass of tea.

"Don't take any drinks from anyone," Millie warned as she sipped her tea.

"Yeah, no kidding." Danielle set her glass on the edge of the desk and peered at the screen. "Wow, there were a lot of keycard entries on deck one this morning. We should try to narrow it down. I would guess the earlier the better since we start our schedule about an hour before most of the other crewmembers."

"Except for the kitchen staff," Millie pointed out.

"Right. I don't think the kitchen crew ever sleeps."

Millie grew quiet as she scrolled through the list searching for "C224," Danielle's cabin number.

"Wait. Back up." Danielle jabbed her finger at the screen. "There. At seven ten this morning. I left at six forty."

"Which means someone may have been waiting for you to leave." Millie double clicked on the keycard entry record and both of them let out a gasp as Tonya Rivera's name popped up.

"Someone is using Tonya's keycard. Oh my gosh. Millie. Someone has access to my cabin."

If Millie was afraid for Danielle before, she was terrified now. "We have to do something."

"Getting me a new keycard won't work."

"You'll need a whole new mechanism, so whoever has Tonya's card won't be able to get in," Millie said.

"You're right, but…" Danielle began to pace.

"But what?"

"That won't help solve the mystery of what happened to Tonya. Let's say Tonya did overdose. Who's to say someone didn't slip drugs into her drink or whatever, especially now that someone left me a note saying 'you're next?'"

"Then a killer gets away with murder," Millie said.

"And I'm still in danger. I can change the access mechanisms on my door and stop whoever has Tonya's keycard from getting in, but it means a killer walks free…and that killer is someone who works on this ship."

"Patterson can handle that."

"Unless he suspects I have Tonya's keycard, used it to access the door and wrote my own threatening note as a way of deflecting suspicion off me." Danielle stopped pacing. "Think about it. I was in the cabin when Tonya died, or right before she died. I had access to her keycard. A prescription bottle was found in my jacket pocket. All of the clues point to me."

"I don't know Danielle…" Millie would never forgive herself if anything happened to Danielle. "What do you propose?"

"I propose we set up some sort of trap to uncover the person or persons who left the note, is using Tonya's keycard and who might be responsible for her death."

"We'll need some help," Millie said. "In the meantime, you're not safe staying at your place."

"Is your offer to let me bunk on your sofa bed still open?"

"Of course. I have to get back to work. Later this evening we'll go to your place together to pack your things and bring them to the apartment." Millie wiggled out of the chair. "Promise me you won't go to your cabin alone."

"I promise," Danielle said. "We still have a couple of suspects to investigate."

"Camille, Tonya's boss and the spa manager," Millie guessed.

"Yep, and Arvin, the non-boyfriend. I have some thoughts on that, but first I think we should visit the spa. I have an idea where Tonya may have stashed either the pills or cash."

The women parted ways outside the bridge, with Danielle promising a second time she wouldn't return to her cabin without Millie.

The rest of the day flew by and Millie completely forgot it was date night and Nic and she were dining in *The Vine* restaurant.

After giving Andy a heads up Nic and she planned a dinner date, Millie made her way to the apartment to freshen up and change.

Nic was already there, sitting at the computer when Millie made her way inside. "You beat me home."

"Vitale knew I was taking you to dinner, so he showed up a little early to start his shift." Nic turned his attention to the computer screen. "I decided to check my email for messages from corporate and found someone left the computer on."

A warm heat crept into Millie's cheeks. "That...was me."

"You logged onto the ship's restricted access site?"

Chapter 11

"I...well. Yes." Millie quickly decided based on the look on her husband's face, she might as well come clean. "Technically, I do have access to specific areas of the site."

"But not all. What were you doing?"

"Checking keycard access." Millie hurried on. "Please don't ask me why."

"Does this have anything to do with the death of Danielle's cabin mate?"

"Yes."

Nic ran a ragged hand through his hair. "I could point out you shouldn't be snooping around in there. A word of warning, the IT department can track anyone who logs onto the site."

"They could, but do they?" Millie hadn't considered that.

"I don't know, but here's your word of warning. If you continue to log onto restricted sites, it will more than likely start throwing up a few red flags and corporate will start asking questions."

"Duly noted and I'm sorry. I'm just trying to help a friend," Millie apologized.

Nic's expression softened. "I know your heart is in the right place. You must be careful though." He slowly stood. "Let's not ruin our date night."

"I agree."

Nic led Scout onto the balcony while Millie ran upstairs to get ready for their date, her husband's words ringing in her ears. There was no way she would ever risk getting him in trouble for her impulsive snooping. Next time, she would ask permission before logging onto the site.

Millie jumped into the shower and made quick work of rinsing off the day's grime. After toweling off, she spritzed on some of her favorite perfume before slipping into one of the sundresses she'd purchase on St. Martin during their honeymoon.

She thought about the plans to visit the spa to try to glean some information from the spa manager about Tonya, and perhaps even some of her co-workers. Nic wouldn't be suspicious of Millie's trip to the spa and she made a mental note to mention it during dinner.

Millie twisted her hair into a loose updo and pulled a few strands free before using her curling iron to create loose ringlets that framed her face. She turned her head to examine the new look. Nodding in approval, she grabbed her new summer sandals and floated down the steps.

Her heart skipped a beat when she caught a glimpse of her husband dressed in his captain's uniform. She caught a whiff of an earthy musk scent and stepped closer. "I better keep a close eye on you tonight lest the female passengers throw themselves at you."

"You know I only have eyes for you." Nic lowered his head and gently kissed his wife's lips. "Our reservations aren't for another hour. I thought we could head downstairs and enjoy the live music in the atrium."

"Perfect," Millie beamed. "I would love to."

Nic held the door and waited for his wife to step onto the bridge before joining her.

Captain Vitale let out a low wolf whistle at the sight of the couple. "You two look ready to paint the town."

"We are. Dinner and dancing." Nic crooked his elbow and Millie slipped her arm through his. "Shall we?"

The couple strolled off the bridge and made their way down to the atrium. The romantic strains of a violin wafted in the air, and they stepped off to the side to watch as several couples circled the dancefloor.

"Shall we?" Nic motioned toward the dancefloor before sweeping his wife into his arms.

Millie quickly forgot about the other guests as Nic and she swayed back and forth to the music. The next song slowed even more and the lights dimmed.

Nic drew her close and a warm flush filled Millie's body as she gazed into her husband's dark, brooding eyes. "If you keep looking at me like that, we might have to skip dinner," Millie whispered breathlessly.

"Really?" Nic lifted a brow, a small smile lifting the corner of his lips. "Don't tempt me."

When the music ended, a flushed Millie took a small step back. The band picked up the tempo and began playing a snappy summer sixties number.

They held hands as Nic led his wife off the dancefloor. A young couple stopped them. "How romantic to be dancing with the ship's captain," the woman gushed.

"He sweeps me off my feet every day." Millie thanked the couple for the compliment and began fanning her face as they walked away. "We should step outside. Is it warm in here or is it just me?"

"You're hot," Nic teased. "I'll buy you a soda at the bar and then we can enjoy a romantic stroll along the promenade deck before heading to *The Vine*."

They carried their drinks outside and slowly meandered along the deck. Off in the distance, Millie spotted a bright cluster of twinkling lights. "Is that another cruise ship?"

"Could be. We won't be alone in St. Martin tomorrow. There are two other ships scheduled to be in port with us."

Millie knew even one ship in port could create large crowds, long lines and traffic delays. Three in port on the same day was almost unbearable, and it was those days where she was content to stay on board the ship.

They circled the promenade before making their way back indoors and up to the sun deck where *The Vine* was located.

The hostess did a double take and saluted Nic while Millie placed a hand over her mouth to hide her smile. She fleetingly wondered what Nic would do if she saluted him.

"Captain Armati, Mrs. Armati...welcome to *The Vine*. We have the best table in the house reserved for you." The hostess led them to a table with floor-to-ceiling windows, offering an unobstructed view of the ocean.

The server hurried over. "Welcome to *The Vine*." She handed each of them a menu, almost spilling Millie's glass of water in the process. "I'm so sorry."

"No worries," Millie smiled warmly as she read the young woman's nametag, *Lisette*.

A young man, who joined Lisette, looked vaguely familiar.

"This is my assistant," Lisette explained. "He will be helping me with this evening's dinner service."

Millie's eyes squinted. "Suri, you're working in *The Vine* now?"

Suri was one of Annette's kitchen workers. She hadn't seen him for several months and wondered what happened to him. She secretly suspected that Annette had kicked him out of her kitchen since he was somewhat scatterbrained.

"Yes, Miss Millie," Suri puffed out his chest. "I work my way up from kitchen to anytime dining room and now I work in *The Vine* with Lisette."

Lisette took the antipasti platter Suri was holding and placed it in the middle of their table. "This is our most popular starter – antipasti. It includes deli meats: salami, spicy capocollo, prosciutto, mortadella, and bresaola."

Lisette pointed to the marinated olives. "The olives…they are very flavorful."

"Spicy?" Millie asked.

"Perhaps. They are made with crushed red pepper flakes. We also have roasted pepper salad with Kalamata olives, fresh basil and fresh garlic."

Lisette stepped to the side. "It is served with freshly baked Italian bread and an olive oil dipping sauce."

Suri placed the basket of bread next to the platter of antipasti.

"It looks delicious," Millie said. "This is the first time Nic and I...er, Captain Armati and I have dined in *The Vine*. I'm not sure I'll want an appetizer with all of this food."

"Oh you must," Lisette insisted. "Even if you don't eat it, you can take it home."

Lisette and Suri took turns rattling off their favorite appetizer. All sounded tempting.

Nic decided to order the arancini, coated in breadcrumbs. Arancini, Nic explained, was a deep fried risotto ball stuffed with cheese and peas and smothered in a red sauce.

Millie ordered something a little lighter, a caprese salad consisting of sliced fresh mozzarella, tomatoes and sweet basil, seasoned with salt and olive oil. Drizzled over the top was balsamic vinegar.

Each ordered San Pellegrino sparkling waters and dug into the delicious antipasti after Lisette and Suri left. While they ate, they discussed the ship's itinerary. Millie confessed she was happy to stay on board the ship in St. Martin.

Nic broke off a large piece of bread and dipped it in the olive oil. "I was thinking it has been some time since we've taken an afternoon off. Perhaps we could squeeze in a few hours in St. Kitts to explore the island."

"Can we?" Millie's eyes lit. The ship's itinerary was new, and the couple hadn't had time to explore the island.

"If you can twist Andy's arm and get a few hours off, I have the perfect day planned," Nic promised.

"That shouldn't be a problem. Andy owes me one." Millie told her husband about Andy's over the top fall festivities and her witch costume. "He even bought one for Scout. He's a hot dog."

Nic burst out laughing. "Now this I have to see. What does Scout think?"

"He took one look at it and backed away."

"Good luck getting him to put it on."

The appetizers arrived and Nic and Millie shared their dishes, declaring them both delicious and a tie.

At Lisette's recommendation, Millie ordered the tortellini in brodo, a northern Italian dish. The tortellini, filled with veal and Parmigiano Reggiano cheese, was served in a homemade chicken broth and topped with a light sprinkling of grated Parmesan.

Nic went for a heartier dish of osso buco alla Milanese, a personal favorite.

"What is it?"

"Veal shanks braised slowly in white wine and vegetables, served with a tangy, garlicky gremolata."

"What is gremolata?"

"It's a chopped herb condiment made with lemon zest, garlic, parsley and anchovy. No dish of osso buco alla Milanese is authentic without it." Nic patted his stomach. "I can't wait to try it. Remind me again why we haven't tried this restaurant before?"

"Because we work all the time," Millie joked.

The dishes arrived not long after Suri removed the appetizer plates. Thankfully, Millie's tortellini dish wasn't nearly as large as Nic's entree.

He sampled his food, claiming it almost as good as his mother's and then offered Millie a taste. She took a small spoonful, thanked him for it and then offered him a tortellini swimming in broth.

He sampled the food, telling her it was good, but could use a little more flavor and then happily returned to devouring his meal.

By the time Millie finished, she was stuffed. She leaned back in her chair and patted her stomach. "That was magnificent and very filling. Maybe I'm glad we don't eat out all of the time."

Suri returned to remove the dinner dishes. "Do you like?"

"The tortellini was delicious, as was the antipasti and the caprese. The bread was warm and crusty. I can't complain about a single thing except I ate too much."

"You will order dessert?"

Millie started to shake her head, but it was too late. Lisette arrived with a tray of tempting desserts. "The tiramisu is delicious. We also have a Sicilian cannoli, an Italian apple tart and chocolate sorbetto."

Nic waited patiently until she finished describing the desserts. "Do you have torrone?"

"It is not on the menu." Lisette realized she was talking to the captain of the ship and quickly explained. "We do have some in the back. I think Chef Ricci is working on adding this to the menu. Let me see if there is any available."

She lowered into a small curtsy before retreating. When she returned moments later, a stout man with dark hair and wearing a tall chef's hat lumbered along behind her.

Nic pushed his chair back and stood. "I didn't mean to drag you out of the kitchen Massimo." He grasped the man's hand in a firm grip.

"I planned to stop by as soon as Lisette let me know you were lingering over coffee and dessert. When she came back and asked if torrone was on the dessert menu, I knew there was only one person who would ask." The man began speaking rapidly in Italian, and Millie only understood a word or two.

Nic answered a brief sentence in turn, and then switched to English. "You have not met my lovely bride, Millie."

The chef beamed as he took Millie's hand and kissed the top. "Ah...all of the rumors of your great beauty do not do you justice." He held her hand a little too long for Millie's liking and she resisted the urge to wipe her hand after he released it.

"You're too kind." His long stare gave her an uncomfortable feeling and she quickly changed the subject. "Thank you for a lovely dinner. Everything was perfect."

"We have the best food on the ship," Massimo Ricci boasted.

Millie almost commented, "other than Annette Delacroix," but now was neither the time nor the place to defend her friend. Instead, she smiled.

"Suri is on his way with a dish of torrone. It is still in the testing stages. I would be appreciative of the feedback."

The chef offered a small bow and then headed back to the kitchen, passing Suri, who was carrying a small covered tray. He set it in the center of the table. "Would you care for coffee or tea?"

"Coffee sounds perfect," Millie said.

"Make it two," Nic added.

Lisette arrived with a pot. She poured two cups and left the carafe on the table.

"You first." Millie motioned to the dish. "I'm stuffed."

Nic lifted the lid. Millie's first thought was it reminded her of fudge, but with a thick layer of toasted nuts in the center.

"Torrone is a creamy candy made with honey, egg whites, toasted nuts and citrus zest. There is another version, dipped in chocolate. This version is true to the original." Nic broke off a piece and bit the end. "It is good."

Millie broke off a piece and nibbled the corner. "It's sweet. I do like the toasted nuts." She finished her piece and sipped her coffee as Nic polished off the rest.

"We managed to eat it all."

"And it was delicious." Nic glanced at his watch. "Sadly, our dinner date has ended. I must work for a few more hours. What is your schedule?"

"Oh." Millie's hand flew to her mouth. "I almost forgot. Danielle is going to camp out on our sofa bed for a couple of nights. I hope you don't mind."

Nic lifted his coffee cup, studying his wife over the rim. "Does this have anything to do with the records you were searching earlier?"

"Maybe," Millie said. "I can't go into detail, but someone threatened Danielle and I don't think it's safe for her to stay in her cabin."

A flicker of concern crossed Nic's face. "You must tell Patterson."

"She won't let me." Millie fiddled with the handle of her coffee cup. "There's more to the story, more to her cabin mate's death. I think Patterson suspects the same. I told her I would give her a day or so. Until then, I think she would be safer staying with us."

Nic studied his wife's face. "I don't agree with this decision not to tell Patterson. We'll wait until tomorrow and then talk to him."

"I...you're right." Millie quietly nodded. "I would never forgive myself if something happened to Danielle."

Suri and Lisette returned to check on them. Nic told them to tell the chef the torrone was delicious, but was missing something. He would give it some thought and get back with him.

The couple wandered out of the restaurant and back to the apartment where Millie switched into her work outfit. She still had several activities to check on before meeting Danielle at her cabin when their shifts ended.

The time flew by and Millie mulled over Nic's words. He was right. Patterson needed to know if a crewmember or staff was being threatened. She vowed to tell him first thing in the morning, after convincing Danielle it was the right thing to do.

By the time Millie reached Danielle's cabin, she'd rehearsed her entire spiel, how she would convince Danielle they needed to tell Patterson.

She found Danielle standing in the hallway, a troubled expression on her face. "Remember how I said I didn't want to tell anyone about the break in and the note? I changed my mind. You'll never guess what I found."

Chapter 12

"Cash?" Millie guessed.

"Nope."

"Drugs?"

"Uh-uh." Danielle shook her head.

"A body?"

Danielle rolled her eyes. "Then I really would need to talk to Patterson. No. Check it out." She motioned Millie inside. "There's a mini camera inside my cabin, hooked to the corner of my television."

"You put a mini camera in your cabin?"

"I didn't put a camera in there. Someone else did. You can see it as plain as day."

Millie reached for the cabin door and Danielle stopped her. "Don't stare directly at it."

"Gotcha." Millie stepped inside, casually glancing around when she caught a glimpse of something round and black perched atop the small corner television.

She returned to the hall and quietly closed the door behind her.

"Did you see it?"

"I saw something, but without crawling on top of the chair and staring at the television, I wasn't able to get a good look."

"Who does that?" Danielle asked.

"A killer."

"A sick, twisted killer who leaves threatening notes. We can still plan a sting, but I think it's time to give Patterson a heads up." Danielle involuntarily shivered. "Just thinking about someone spying on me makes me want to throw up."

"Which is another reason why you need to pack up your things and stay with me until the culprit is caught." Millie lowered her voice. "What if there's a voice recording device, too?"

"If there is…" Danielle raised her voice, "I'm coming after you sicko. You aren't getting away with this."

Danielle threw the cabin door open and marched inside. She pulled her backpack out of the closet and began shoving clothes into it before moving on to the dresser where she tossed more things inside.

"That should do it. Now all I need is my toothbrush." She darted into the bathroom while Millie gazed anxiously around the room.

What if there was another camera…one that Danielle missed? She took a tentative step forward and peered at the curtain, giving it a gentle tug.

She moved on to the bunks, careful to stay out of the camera's line of vision as she casually lifted the mattresses and ran her hand along the edge.

"What are you doing?"

Millie jumped, clutching her chest as she spun around. "You scared me."

"Sorry. What are you doing?" Danielle repeated.

"Checking for more cameras or recording devices."

"I already searched the place. It's clean." Danielle snapped her fingers. "I've got a brilliant idea. Let's step into the hall."

She waited until Millie closed the door behind them. "What if we turn the tables by setting up our own surveillance camera and catching them in the act?"

"I like the idea, but where are we gonna find a camera?" Millie asked.

"Annette."

"Ahh. I hadn't thought about her. Before we do anything, I want to talk to Patterson to let him know what's going on."

The women made their way to the security office. The lights were on. When they stepped inside, they found Oscar instead of Patterson.

"Is Patterson around?" Danielle asked.

"He's gone for the night. I'm covering the night shift. Is there something I can help you with?"

"As a matter of fact," Millie said.

"No. We'll wait and talk to him tomorrow." Danielle grabbed Millie's hand and dragged her out of the office. "Oscar won't be able to do much. We need to talk to Patterson. I say we track Annette down and set a trap."

"I dunno…" Millie eyed her friend.

"C'mon," Danielle said.

"Against my better judgment…okay, but if Annette's gone for the night, we let it go until tomorrow."

"It's a deal."

When the women reached the galley, Millie was relieved to see the lights were off. "It looks like we'll have to wait. Let's head home."

Millie started to walk past, but Danielle wasn't following. "I see a small light on in the back. I think someone is still in there." She pressed lightly on the swinging door and it opened. "See? You give up too easily."

Danielle disappeared inside the galley and Millie reluctantly followed.

"Hello? Annette?" Danielle called out.

The dim light grew brighter. "Miss Annette, she gone for the day." It was Amit.

"Amit, what are you doing here this late at night?" Millie asked.

"I finish cleaning up. The other kitchen, the one that handles the late night buffet and room service, the fryers not working, so I let them use our kitchen until maintenance get it fixed."

"That was nice of you, Amit," Millie said.

"Miss Annette say if I stay, I don't have to come to work until later tomorrow."

"I'm sure you're anxious to get out of here." Millie turned to go. "Have a good night."

Danielle lifted her arm, almost clotheslining Millie. "Wait! Amit, do you know if Miss Annette keeps some of her spy supplies in the kitchen?"

"Spy supplies?" Amit asked.

"Recording devices, cameras, her special mirrored spy glasses, you know, her spy stuff," Danielle said.

"Ah." Amit smiled. "She does keep a few items in her office."

The women followed him to the dry goods storage closet, aka Annette's office.

Amit reached for a tin, labeled *baking powder*. He removed the lid before handing it to Millie. "Everything is in here."

Millie stuck her hand inside and pulled out a small video recording device. Next, she pulled out a thin strip of wire attached to a handful of flash drives. "What are these for? Nevermind. Maybe I don't want to know."

She reached in a third time and then handed Danielle a small square piece of plastic. "This might do the trick. What do you think?"

Danielle turned it over. "We'll need to make sure there's a micro SD card for recording. Ah...I see it there. I wonder if it's charged."

"Yes." Amit's head bobbed up and down. "It is. Miss Annette, she keep all of her baking powder charged."

"Sweet," Danielle squealed. "Do you think she'll mind if we borrow it?"

Amit glanced at Danielle and then Millie. "No. I think Miss Annette won't mind. If she does, I will take the blame."

Millie patted his arm. "No you won't, Amit. I will take the blame."

"We better get a move on." Danielle slipped the small device into her jacket pocket. "We owe you one, Amit."

Amit followed them to the door. "Good luck."

"Thanks. Hopefully, this will help solve a mystery or two."

Danielle and Millie returned to Danielle's cabin and stopped in the outer hall. "We need to place it somewhere inconspicuous."

"And also somewhere out of view of the other camera," Millie added.

"Let me think for a minute." Danielle tapped her foot on the floor. "I've got it. I'll hook it to the top of the trash can, under the desk. You'll need to create some sort of diversion while I crawl under the desk and hook it up."

"A diversion?"

"Right. I'm sure you'll think of something," Danielle said confidently as she slipped her keycard in the slot and pushed the door open.

Millie entered the cabin first, making a point not to look directly at the camera. She grabbed the television remote and began flipping through the channels. "News, weather, a rerun of the headliner show the other night," she muttered under her breath. She stopped when she found a channel with a yoga class in session.

"This might work." Millie lifted her arms as she imitated the instructor's pose. Placing one foot in front of her, she balanced on her back leg as she leaned into a forward stretch. Her back made a small popping noise.

Millie's legs began to shake. "Hurry *up*," she hissed at the television. "My body can't handle too many of these pretzel stretches." She could hear a rustling sound and then Danielle brushed against the side of her leg as she crawled under the desk.

The instructor stretched out on the mat and bent forward, grasping her ankles with both hands and bending low. Millie couldn't draw attention to the floor, so she faked a move, lifting her hands above her head and tilting her head back. There was another small snap, this time in her neck. "You better hurry before I end up in traction," she gasped breathlessly.

Millie thought she heard Danielle giggle and resisted the urge to jab her with her foot. The stretch deepened and she could feel Danielle slip past her again.

"Mission accomplished."

"Help!" Millie groaned as she teetered back and forth. "This pose is giving me body betrayal."

Danielle sprang forward and grabbed hold of Millie's midsection to steady her.

"Thanks." Millie's legs trembled as she straightened to a more natural position. "Remind me not to try that move again. Well? Did it work?"

"We'll find out soon enough." Danielle slung her backpack over her shoulder. "I don't know about you, but all of this sleuthing wore me out. I'm ready to hit the hay."

Danielle followed Millie into the hall and pulled the door shut behind them. "Tomorrow should be a piece of cake since it's a port day. We're still going to check out the spa, right?"

"Yes, after we talk to Patterson," Millie reminded her.

"I wanna get up a little early tomorrow to come down here and check the camera. My gut tells me whoever it is won't show up tonight. I'm guessing they'll do it early in the morning, after they think I started my shift."

"Maybe not. Maybe whoever it is plans to come back tonight to follow through on their threat," Millie said. "Which is why we need to talk to Patterson, the sooner the better."

"We will."

When they reached the bridge, Nic was still working. He chatted with them briefly and told them he would be another hour.

Scout, completely recovered from his busy day, greeted them at the door.

Millie picked him up. "I'll take Scout out and then we'll set up the bed."

"Cool." Danielle dropped her backpack on what would be her bed and followed Millie and Scout onto the balcony. She leaned over the railing and closed her eyes. "You're lucky, Millie. I would love to have a balcony, or even a porthole."

"It is nice," Millie admitted. "Sometimes I feel guilty, knowing all of you are below deck in cramped cabins while I'm up here enjoying this luxurious apartment."

Danielle's eyes flew open. "I didn't say it to make you feel guilty, Millie. I meant…"

"I know you didn't."

"I adore my little cabin. It's cozy and quiet. With great gifts come great responsibilities," Danielle said.

"Wise words," Millie smiled. "Now let's get in there and make your bed. I'm whupped."

The women made quick work of setting up the bed. Millie showed Danielle around the downstairs bathroom and kitchen and told her to make herself at home.

Finally, Millie trudged up the stairs. She had just finished getting ready for bed when Nic joined her. "How is Danielle?"

"I think she's quite comfortable, at least that's my guess since she's snoring. Scout refused to leave Danielle's side, so I left him downstairs."

"She needs a good night's rest." Millie sat up in bed. "Thank you for letting her stay with us."

"You're welcome. Have you thought anymore about speaking with Patterson about Danielle's situation?" Nic asked.

"Yes. Danielle and I are going to track him down first thing tomorrow morning. She found a camera device in her cabin, attached to the top of the television."

"You're kidding? Someone broke into her cabin and placed a camera inside?"

"Not broke in. Whoever it was had a key…Tonya's key."

The statement gained Nic's full attention. "Had I known that, I would have insisted we track Patterson down this evening and tell him what's going on."

"I know." Millie placed a light hand on her husband's arm. "We already tried. He was gone for the day. Like I said, we're going to talk to him in the morning. In the meantime, she's safe here with us."

"Yes, she is." Nic pulled Millie close. "Now if you're not too tired after our romantic date night and all of your snooping and sleuthing, I think I would like to collect on a promise you made earlier."

Chapter 13

Millie woke with a start early the next morning. Her eyes flew open and she stared into the darkness.

A muffled thump echoed from downstairs, reminding her Danielle was camped out on their sofa bed.

She slid out of bed and tiptoed to the bathroom. By the time she emerged, Nic was awake. "Did I sleep through the alarm?" he asked groggily.

Millie glanced at the bedside clock. "No. You have another ten minutes. I woke up a little early and figured I might as well get started." She carried her shoes to the bed and sat on the edge as she slipped them on.

"Did you sleep well?" Nic began rubbing her back.

"Yes. After my dreamy date with my hunky husband and a little romance to top it off, I slept like a baby." Millie ran her hand along Nic's morning stubble.

"Me too." Nic captured her hand and kissed the palm. "But alas, it's time to get up and focus on docking in Philipsburg."

"I'm going downstairs. I think I heard Danielle moving around." Millie stood. "I'm sure Scout woke her up already."

"I'll be down shortly." Nic disappeared inside the bathroom, and Millie wandered downstairs. The light above the stove was on and she caught a whiff of freshly brewed coffee.

When she reached the bottom, she spotted Danielle and Scout standing out on the balcony. "Hey, Danielle."

"Good morning, Millie." Danielle held up her coffee cup. "I hope you don't mind. I found the coffee and started a pot."

"Not at all. Let me grab a cup. I'll be right back." Millie joined her friend, balancing the cup on the railing. "How did you sleep?"

"I was out like a light. I don't remember waking up until Scout trounced across my chest and refused to leave me alone. We've only been up for about half an hour or so."

Scout, hearing his name, trotted across the balcony and pounced on Millie's shoe. "You're a stinker. No wonder you wanted to stay downstairs with Danielle."

"I found Scout's food in the cupboard, so I fed him and gave him some fresh water."

"That was nice of you. Did you find the coffee cake on top of the fridge?"

"No. That's sounds good." Danielle lifted her cup. "I'm going in for a refill and a piece of cake. Would you like one?"

"No thanks." Millie waited for Danielle to leave before shifting her gaze to the shoreline off in the distance.

"I'm leaving."

Millie turned at the sound of her husband's voice. "You look dapper this morning."

Nic stepped out onto the balcony. "And you look beautiful." He tugged on a strand of Millie's hair. "I like your longer hair. Maybe you shouldn't cut it."

"Maybe I shouldn't." Millie bounced up on her tiptoes for a good-bye kiss and reluctantly watched as Nic stepped back inside. She heard the front door close moments later, and Danielle rejoined her.

"You have a hot husband." Danielle let out a low whistle.

"He's the best thing that ever happened to me, besides my children and grandchildren." Millie's cheeks warmed as she thought about last night. "Sometimes I want to pinch myself to make sure I'm not dreaming."

Danielle took a big bite of the sweet breakfast treat. "I figure if we hurry up and get ready, we can swing by my place to swap out the reader card and see if the hidden camera caught anyone."

"Afterwards, we're going to stop by Patterson's office to let him know what's going on," Millie said. "By then, it will be time for me to meet Andy at the gangway."

The women split up with Millie returning upstairs to make the bed while Danielle made a beeline for the downstairs bathroom. After finishing, they met in the kitchen to compare their work schedules for the day.

"What does your schedule look like this afternoon, say around one-thirty?" Danielle asked. "We can visit the spa."

"That will be perfect. I'm kicking off the fall movie marathon down in the theater at one," Millie frowned. "Great."

"Great what?"

"Andy scribbled a note next to the movie marathon...costume required."

"Don't feel bad. Andy expects me to wear the clown costume to the kid's haunted house. The kids won't even have to go inside the haunted house to get scared. They'll take one look at me and start screaming."

"Did you point out to him kids hate clowns?"

"Yeah. I don't think he believed me. He will, once the parents start complaining," Danielle said. "So we're going to meet in front of the spa at one-thirty?"

"Sounds good."

Millie rinsed their cups in the sink while Danielle let Scout out for one more potty break. The women exited the apartment, making their way to Danielle's cabin to drop off her belongings and check the surveillance camera. At first glance, it appeared no one had disturbed it during the night.

Danielle found her surveillance camera still in place and quickly swapped out the reader card, slipping the one she removed into her pocket. With a quick check of the cabin, the women stepped back into the hall and made their way to the security office.

Although it was early, the lights were on and the women made their way inside. Patterson was sitting at his desk with Oscar on the other side.

"You're still here?" Millie asked Oscar. "Don't you ever sleep?"

"I'm finishing my shift." Oscar stood.

"You can stay, Oscar. This won't take long." Millie turned to Danielle. "You tell them."

"Someone has been sneaking into my cabin. I found a spy camera hidden above my television and a note on the floor." Danielle dropped the note on Patterson's desk.

Patterson read the note and then handed it to Oscar. "You say you found a surveillance camera in your cabin?"

"Yes. We left it there, hoping whoever put it there would come back."

"You want someone to break into your cabin?"

"There's a reason..." Millie prompted.

"We set up a spy camera of our own."

"You did?" Patterson leaned back in his chair. "Where did you get a surveillance camera?"

"We borrowed it – from a friend. Millie and I swapped out the reader card on our way here. We haven't looked at it yet." Danielle set the small reader device on the desk.

Patterson turned to Oscar. "We need to check the staff keycard access records to find out who has been inside Danielle's cabin."

"We already know," Millie said quietly. "Please don't ask me how."

"Why am I not surprised?" Patterson sighed heavily. "Okay. For the sake of an argument, I'm not going to ask you how you know. Who was it?"

"Someone using Tonya's access card," Millie said.

Oscar and Patterson exchanged a quick glance.

"You already knew Tonya's keycard was missing," Danielle said. "Why didn't you come back to take another look around?"

"We did, and we've been monitoring access to her cabin, but it appears whoever it was slipped by. There are hundreds of keycard entries at any given time and difficult to track them all."

Millie made eye contact with Patterson. "Did you plant the spy camera?"

"No." Patterson shook his head. "We did not plant a spy camera. After our initial search, when we couldn't locate Tonya's keycard, we searched the cabin again, but couldn't find it."

"You do suspect I had something to do with Tonya's death. My life could be in danger and you don't even care." Danielle's face was a mask of fury. She stormed out of Patterson's office, slamming the door behind her.

Millie cringed at the loud bang. "It would have been a little more helpful if you let Danielle at least be there during your search. Someone on board this ship is using her dead cabin mate's keycard to sneak in."

"I'll be the first to admit, I haven't handled this as I should. Danielle was…is a suspect. She had both motive and opportunity to take Tonya out."

"What about the drugs?" Millie pointed out. "The drugs delivered to the ship with Tonya's name on them?"

It was Patterson's turn to look surprised. "Who told you that?"

Millie could feel her blood pressure rise. "I see what's going on. You suspect Tonya and Danielle were both dealing prescription drugs, something went wrong and Danielle took Tonya out, but not before Tonya planted a bottle in Danielle's work jacket."

Patterson's silence at Millie's statement was all of the answer she needed. She turned to follow her friend out of the office when she spotted the card reader on the desk.

Millie snatched it off the desk and stomped out of the office.

Vowing to clear Danielle's name and prove Patterson wrong, she made a beeline for the galley. Millie found Annette standing in front of the stove. "Hey, Annette."

"Hi, Millie." Annette turned, spatula in hand. "You look like you just lost your best friend."

"Worse, Patterson believes Danielle is responsible for Tonya's death, someone is sneaking into Danielle's cabin and she might quit."

The whole story tumbled out and by the time Millie finished, she was relieved to have the sordid mess off her chest.

"That is a mess. Poor Danielle feels betrayed by Patterson and rightfully so."

"We have to figure out who murdered Tonya and is threatening Danielle." Millie slipped her hand into her pocket, her fingertips touching the small card reader. "We borrowed your surveillance camera to try to catch the culprit sneaking into Danielle's cabin, but haven't had time to check it yet."

"No time like the present." Annette darted to the dry goods storage room and returned carrying an iPad.

"I didn't know you owned an iPad," Millie said.

"I picked it up a coupla months ago. Got tired of lugging my laptop around and figured this would be easier to transport and store." She plugged the reader adapter into the iPad and then popped the reader card into the side slot.

"Haven't used it much since I bought it, mostly to spy on the kitchen crew to make sure they're doing their job when I'm not around." Annette began tapping the screen. "We got something."

Millie hurried to her friend's side and peered over Annette's shoulder. Although the image was a little grainy, she could make out the outline of a person sneaking inside.

From the angle of Danielle's hidden camera, the view was of the lower portion of the person's body. A bright flash of light indicated the intruder had stepped into the bathroom. It went dark.

"I bet they snuck in to swap out the reader card," Millie whispered.

"You don't have to whisper. There isn't any sound," Annette whispered back.

"Right." Millie's pulse ticked up a notch as the person returned to the main cabin and walked right toward the camera.

Chapter 14

"Let's back it up a frame." Annette fiddled with the screen and enlarged the picture. "Crud."

"Crud is right." The intruder was wearing a dark hoodie. Millie couldn't tell if the person was male or female. Moments later, they slipped out of the cabin and shut the door behind them.

The women watched the video again, noting the time. The footage was taken at six ten that morning. "Whoever it is, knows Danielle's schedule."

"You better let her stay with you until this loser is caught." Annette wiggled the reader card out of the slot and dropped it in Millie's hand. "I suggest you swap the reader card out again later tonight, before you turn in and keep checking for activity."

"Thanks, Annette. Danielle, Cat and I are going to do a little investigative work in the spa after lunch to see if we can get a feel for Tonya and her relationship with her co-workers and boss."

The galley floor gently vibrated as the ship shuddered. "The ship is docking. I better grab a bite to eat before heading downstairs to meet Andy at the gangway."

"Take some pumpkin crunch cake with you. I made another batch and tweaked the recipe. You can let me know what you think later." Annette sliced two thick pieces of cake before placing each piece on a napkin and handing them to Millie.

"Thanks for the yummy treats and everything else." Millie impulsively hugged her friend and then darted out into the hall.

With a quick stop for more coffee and a piece of fruit, Millie reached the gangway at the same time as Andy, who was coming from the opposite direction.

Andy pointed at the crunch cake. "That looks tasty."

"It's delicious. Annette made it. Have a piece." Millie handed him the second piece.

"Wow." Andy polished it off in one big bite. "Annette is doing a bang-up job with the fall recipes."

"Speaking of fall, I'm thinking of skipping the witch costume this afternoon."

"Millie…" The look Andy gave her meant he was serious about the costume.

"Fine. Have it your way. For the record, I protest."

The first wave of guests, on their way out for early shore excursions, began exiting the ship.

"Is it just me or does it seem like everyone is getting off?"

"Almost all of the shore excursions sold out before we left Miami," Andy said. "In fact, the excursions were so popular we added a couple extra.

My guess is most of our guests are getting off today. It should be a fairly quiet day on board."

Finally, the crowds thinned. "If you can stay a little longer, I would like to check on Danielle," Andy said.

Warning bells rang in Millie's head. She hadn't chatted with her friend since Danielle stormed out of Patterson's office early that morning. "She's upset with Patterson."

"I heard. I think she'll be all right as long as she doesn't have to meet with Patterson again until after the investigation is wrapped up."

Millie nodded absentmindedly. "She's understandably upset. I can see her side. I can see Patterson's side. He's doing his job. The evidence points to Danielle. Somehow, we have to clear her name." She almost mentioned the video footage, how she and Danielle planned to visit the spa and talk to Tonya's co-workers, but decided to keep quiet.

She watched Andy walk away and then turned her attention to a group of passengers who wanted to know where to pick up the shuttle boat that ferried visitors from the port to Philipsburg.

Finally, the gangway area cleared and Millie tried radioing Danielle, who never answered.

Millie's first official event of the day was hosting a round of trivia. There was still time before the scheduled start. She drifted aimlessly around the ship and found herself near the entrance to the Sky Chapel.

It had been at least a month since Millie last visited the chapel, mostly because her schedule didn't permit. She tiptoed to the front of the dark sanctuary and eased onto the steps.

Sudden tears burned the back of her eyes as she lowered her head to pray. She prayed for Danielle, she prayed for Tonya and her family, she prayed for her own family and loved ones.

A lone tear trickled down her cheek as she lifted her head and she quickly swiped it away. It had been a long time since she'd cried. This time, it was for her young friend.

Danielle lost a brother and rarely spoke of family back home. What would Danielle do if she left the Siren of the Seas? What about her relationship with Brody?

Millie slowly stood. She stared at the cross for a long moment, reminding herself Jesus loved Danielle more than anyone else ever could. He would take care of Millie's young friend.

A sense of peace washed over Millie as she wandered out of the chapel and stepped back into the stifling hot Caribbean heat. It was time for Millie to get back to work.

*****

"You're a witch." A young boy pinched Millie's wart-covered rubber nose and ran off.

Millie sighed heavily as she scratched her arm. The costume was hot and she was starting to sweat.

Half the passengers who showed up for the movie marathon complimented her on her costume while the rest laughed.

Her co-host, one of the ship's dancers, repeated several times how glad he was Andy hadn't forced him to wear a costume.

Each time she got a jeer or laugh, Millie silently vowed Andy would pay dearly for the getup. Finally, after handing out dozens of bags of popcorn and cans of soda, along with printouts of the movie schedule, she traipsed back to the apartment to change out of the costume.

Nic was on the bridge. He did a double take when he saw his wife's outfit and a slow smile crept across his face.

"Don't even go there," Millie warned. "This was Andy's crummy idea and I'm plotting my revenge."

"You look adorable." Nic crossed the bridge and gently patted the offensive wart nose. "Even with the warts."

"You're lying. This costume is a train wreck. Half the people felt sorry for me...the other half laughed. I'm never wearing this again," Millie vowed.

Nic was still smiling as Millie made her way into the apartment. Scout was waiting near the door. He took one look at the witch outfit, let out a small whimper and took off.

"I don't blame you." Millie couldn't get the costume off fast enough. She had half a mind to toss it over the side of the ship, but while she was changing, she came up with an even better idea.

She carefully folded the cape, placing it back in the bag, on top of the pointed black shoes. The nose was next, followed by the witch's hat. "We'll just see about this."

She slid the bag into the hall closet and then took Scout out for a break. The afternoon sun had shifted and was beating down on the balcony. Scout was quick to take care of business and promptly returned to the cool apartment air.

By the time Millie reached the spa for their fact-finding mission, Cat was already there waiting. "No Danielle?"

"Not yet."

Danielle arrived a short time later, out of breath, her cheeks flushed.

"What happened to you?"

"I was wearing the stupid clown costume while we were working out the kinks in the haunted house and a teenager attacked me. He ripped my wig off and I had to chase him down to get it back. Wait until I get my hands on Andy."

"Me too." Millie told her about her humiliating experience outside the theater, how half of the people made fun of her. "It was mostly the younger passengers. I think the adults felt sorry for me."

"We need to figure out a way to pay Andy back for this nonsense," Danielle said.

"I agree, but first we have some sleuthing to do." The women trailed behind Millie as she led the way to the spa's front desk.

The woman behind the desk, *Joy,* according to her nametag, smiled hesitantly. "Hello."

Millie flashed her identification card. "Yes. I'm Millie Armati, Assistant Cruise Director. This is my co-worker, Danielle. You may already know Cat, who works in the gift shop."

"Hi, Joy."

The woman smiled. "It's nice to see you, Cat."

"We've been getting a lot of questions lately from guests inquiring about the spa experience," Millie said. "Since we don't know much about it, we figured this afternoon would be the perfect opportunity to take a tour and learn more about your services, so we can give the passengers helpful information."

"Of course. That's a great idea." The woman reached behind the counter and handed each of them a stack of brightly colored pamphlets. "This lists all of the services available. We even offer acupuncture."

Danielle giggled and Millie frowned. "I know all about the acupuncture services thanks to my boss."

Joy continued. "I would be happy to give you a tour, but there's no one here to watch the front desk."

Danielle glanced around. "Is the spa manager here?"

"Camille Bessette is the spa manager. She's on break right now, but will be returning shortly. Perhaps by the time you finish touring the facility, she'll be back and can cover anything you might have missed."

"That sounds perfect," Cat said. "We're sorry about your co-worker, Tonya's death. Such a sad situation."

A flicker crossed Joy's face. She quickly recovered. "Yes. We were all shocked to hear the news. She and Camille were close friends."

"Were you and Tonya friends, as well?" Millie asked.

"No." Joy shook her head. "We typically worked different shifts, only passing by with a quick 'hello' once in a while. The investigators have been up here asking a lot of questions, mostly about Camille."

Joy glanced over Millie's shoulder and a faint smile flickered across her face. "Hi, Rachel."

Millie turned to face Rachel Quaid, the ship's nurse. She moved to the side to make room. "Hello, Millie, Danielle." She turned her attention to Joy.

"Is Stephen here?"

"He's in his office," Joy said. "Is your back still giving you trouble?"

"It seems to be getting worse. I haven't been able to bend over for days." Rachel grabbed her back. "If

I can't get any relief soon, I may have to try a chiropractor."

"I'll give Doctor Chow a call to let him know you're here." Joy picked up the phone while Rachel gave them a nod and limped down the hall.

"Better her than me," Danielle muttered under her breath.

Millie thanked the woman, and they headed to the set of doors on the right that opened to a long hall. On each side were more doors, some with signs that said "in session."

"I say we bypass the session ones and check out the others," Danielle suggested.

The women made their way down the hall, stopping to peek inside several of them. The rooms were small and Millie could hear soft music playing in the background.

They strolled to the end of the hall and turned right toward the double doors marked "Sauna."

After inspecting the sauna room, they returned to the hall. On the opposite side was a door marked, "Showers."

"Shall we?" Danielle said.

"Leave no stone unturned, or in this case, no door unopened," Millie joked as she and Cat followed Danielle inside.

The clean scent of lemon, mixed with bleach permeated the room. To the left was a row of restroom stalls. To the right was a row of lockers.

The trio passed by the restroom and locker area, making their way to the shower area.

"These are nice," Cat said. "I was in here a long time ago and the showers weren't nearly as nice as they are now."

The spacious showers boasted overhead rain showers and rich brown tiles. In front of each stall was a large white curtain. Beyond the curtains were frosted glass doors.

Danielle reached inside and grabbed a fistful of toiletries. "Look at all of the high-end toiletries you get to use. I should start showering in here."

"The showers are nice," Millie admitted. They were even nicer than the shower in the apartment's master bathroom. "Before we leave, we should try to snag a few sample spa products."

"Maybe Joy has trial size samples we can offer for sale in Ocean Treasures," Cat said.

After examining each of the bathroom stalls, the showers and the lockers, the women exited the area.

"What do you think about Rachel Quaid and Stephen Chow?" Danielle asked.

"Maybe she's one of those women who likes pain," Millie turned to Cat. "Has Joe…Doctor Gundervan mentioned Rachel and Chow being an item?"

"Nope." Cat shook her head. "If Rachel and Chow are dating, they're keeping it on the down low. I'm going to casually mention it to Joe and see what he says."

"See?" Millie patted Cat's shoulder. "Maybe Rachel and Joe weren't sneaking around behind your back, after all."

"I wouldn't put anything past Rachel. Maybe she's after both of them."

The women began making their way back to the front when Millie spotted another door she hadn't noticed earlier, marked *Spa Staff Only*.

She glanced around to make sure they were alone. "Check it out." She jabbed her finger at the sign on the door.

"Oh...I don't think we should go in there." Cat took a step back.

"Why not?" Danielle reached for the doorknob.

"It says 'Spa Staff Only.'"

"That has never stopped us before."

Chapter 15

Millie squinted her eyes at the narrow beam of light filtering in from a small, twelve-inch porthole. "I can't see a thing." She took a step forward and collided with Cat.

"Ouch!"

"Sorry."

"We better hurry before someone catches us." Danielle crept across the room to the beverage station where a Keurig coffee maker sat next to a tidy stack of ceramic mugs. She picked one up. "I like this mug." In big, bold turquoise letters were the words, *Serenity Spa*.

While Danielle scoped out the beverage station, Millie sifted through the color-coded files on the opposite wall. "Someone is super organized." She turned at the sound of clanging metal. "What are you doing?"

"I'm trying to open these lockers." Cat tapped one of the locks. "Maybe one of them belonged to Tonya."

"I bet you're right." Danielle set the mug down and joined Cat. "I can pick the lock."

"With what...your fingernail?" Millie teased. "Besides, these are combination locks."

"Hmm..." Danielle grabbed the nearest lock and began spinning the dials. "Rats."

"It could be a million different combinations." Millie eyed the door nervously. "We don't have all day."

"Hold your horses. I have an idea." Danielle pulled hard on the bottom of the lock and began slowly spinning the first dial until she heard a faint click. "It works. I think I can open this."

A sudden commotion outside the door made Millie jump. Before she could dive for cover, the door flew open. *"What are you doing in here?"*

Cat leapt in front of Danielle, blocking the view. "We...uh. We thought this was the locker room and wanted to check it out."

Camille, the spa manager, motioned to the sign on the door. "This area is for employees only. The guest lockers are down the hall."

The women retreated to the hall, walking single file, as they passed Camille who eyed them suspiciously. "How did you get in here? The door was supposed to be locked."

"It wasn't," Danielle insisted. "We walked right in."

"We're sorry. We had no idea. I'm glad you explained that to us." Cat attempted to smooth things over. "I was telling Danielle and Millie I think it would be a great idea to set up a spa product display inside the *Ocean Treasures* gift shop."

Camille's expression softened. "My staff and I were discussing ways to increase the spa's visibility. We include flyers with the *Cruise Ship Chronicles* almost every day, but the flyers are competing with other offers, including the gift shop, and most of the passengers just toss them in the trash without ever looking at them."

Cat fell into step with Camille while Millie and Danielle followed. "We could set out a few of your best selling products, so the shoppers can sample them."

"That would be great," Camille gushed. "We don't make much on our services, but we make a decent commission on products we sell."

Cat and Camille talked shop on the way back to the front of the spa. When they reached the front desk, Camille promised to stop by the gift shop to drop off a display and sample goods later that afternoon.

"I think it's an excellent idea," Millie chimed in. "I was wondering if I could get a copy of the spa's hours. I know it's posted in the daily schedule, but with tons of other events to choose from, it tends to get lost in the shuffle."

Before Camille could answer, Joy handed Millie a small stack of sheets. "Here are our spa hours."

"Thank you." Millie took a quick glance at the top sheet and tucked them inside her jacket pocket. You have a lovely spa. Another idea is to start passing out discount cards to our trivia winners."

"I can have Joy print some up," Camille said. "Do you think a twenty-five percent discount would work?"

"I don't know. We could start with that and if no one redeems them maybe up the amount," Millie said.

"I…I'm sorry I snapped at you earlier," Camille apologized. "We're all a little on edge around here. Someone broke into our breakroom the other night. I think security may have scared them off. Nothing was missing, but whoever it was tore the place apart."

"That's the first time we've ever had someone break in," Joy said. "We've been extra cautious making sure everything is locked since the incident."

"Except for today."

"Do you lock the showers and sauna?" As far as Millie knew, both were open 24/7, available for those who wanted to use the gym or sauna, which was free for all cruise ship passengers.

"No. The main areas are open all of the time. It could have been anyone," Camille said.

"Even a guest?" Danielle asked.

"I suppose," Camille shrugged. "Why would a guest break into the staff only area?"

"To steal your products," Cat guessed.

"I'm sorry to hear about the break-in," Millie said. "And I'm sorry we scared you."

"It's okay. Between the break-in and my employee's unexpected death, we've had a tough week around here."

"I can only imagine." Danielle guessed Camille didn't know she was Tonya's cabin mate and quickly decided it was best to keep the information to herself, at least for now.

The trio thanked Joy and Camille, who promised she would stop by the *Ocean Treasures* to drop off the display goods and Millie's discount coupons by the end of the day.

Millie remained quiet until they were out of the spa and on the open deck. "Well? What do you think?"

"I think we need to find out what's inside those employee lockers," Cat said. "Did you see how Camille reacted when she saw us?"

"She was freaked out," Danielle said. "You heard her. Someone broke into the breakroom and tore the place apart."

"A hundred bucks says whoever broke in is also the same person who left the surveillance camera and note in Danielle's cabin," Millie said. "If Camille is right and security scared off the intruder, they'll be back."

"And we have to beat them to it," Cat said.

"Maybe it was Camille who trashed the employee breakroom," Millie theorized. "To make it look like an intruder broke in. Maybe it was really an inside job."

"We'll need to come up with a new strategy for going back in." Danielle clenched her fists. "We need to do it ASAP, before whoever broke in makes a return visit."

"This should be easy." Millie pulled out the small stack of papers Joy had given her. "I'm one step ahead of you, gals. That's why I asked Camille for the spa hours."

"Way to go, Millie." Danielle lifted her sleeve and flexed her muscles. "I say we wait until later this evening, after the spa closes, and spend a little time in the gym pumping some iron."

After consulting their schedules for the rest of the day, the women agreed to meet in the gym at ten-thirty, after the second headliner show ended.

Although the gift shop would still be open, Cat assured them she would have a worker cover for her.

The rest of the afternoon passed in a blur. Millie devoured her sandwich from the deli before starting her afternoon trivia. By the time the second headliner show ended, Millie was beginning to regret their plan to sneak back into the spa breakroom. What if they ran into whoever was after Danielle…the hooded stranger caught on video inside her cabin?

She was the last to arrive at the gym. Danielle and Cat were already there waiting for her.

"Are you okay?" Cat asked. "You look stressed out."

"I'm getting a bad feeling about this," Millie said. "What if we run into the hooded intruder we caught on camera? What if Camille shows up and catches us again?"

"Don't worry about Camille." Cat waved dismissively. "She stopped by earlier with the products and display. Oh. I have your discount coupons." She pulled a banded stack of coupons from her bra and handed them to Millie.

"What on earth?"

"I didn't have anywhere else to put them," Cat said.

"Neither do I." Millie patted her sweatpants.

"No problem." Cat replaced the coupons. "Don't forget to remind me to give them to you later."

"Okay," Millie laughed. "So what's the plan?"

"We work out for a few minutes and then head to the showers, making a slight detour along the way." Danielle gave them a thumbs up. "Let's roll."

Millie wandered over to the treadmill and gave it the once over before turning it on low speed and stepping onto the track. She was just getting into the swing of things when Danielle circled the treadmill, giving Millie a frantic look.

"What's wrong?"

"You'll never guess who just walked in."

Chapter 16

Millie kept a tight grip on the treadmill's handlebar and attempted to glance over her shoulder. "Patterson?"

"Arvin."

"Arvin?"

"Arvin Kurtz, Tonya's non-boyfriend. The one she was hanging around before her death."

"Ah. The one she also worked with on board the Marquise of the Seas."

"Bingo. He works downstairs in recycling. I wonder what he's doing up here," Danielle whispered.

"Picking up trash?"

"No. Something's fishy." Danielle walked to the front of the treadmill and pivoted on her heel. "I think he's looking for something or someone. We need to follow him."

Millie had a sudden thought. What if Arvin was the one who broke into the spa employee breakroom? It made perfect sense…the fact he and Tonya worked together on board the other cruise ship. The two were seeing each other. Was it possible Arvin was selling the prescription drugs to the ship's crewmembers?

She voiced her thoughts. "What if Tonya and Arvin weren't an item, but business partners instead? Tonya could have easily slipped in other deliveries when she picked up the spa packages. No one would pay attention."

Danielle picked up. "Since he worked mostly below deck, he would have an easy market for the pills."

"And maybe even spa employees," Millie added. "It's possible something went wrong, the two of them argued and Arvin took her out."

"I'm sure Tonya mentioned to him she and I couldn't stand each other. What better scheme to get away with murder than to frame the roommate?"

"Which could be why there was a prescription bottle in your pocket, planted by the person who took Tonya's keycard."

"But why keep sneaking into my cabin?" Danielle asked.

"Maybe he's looking for money or pills. The intruder, possibly Arvin, thinks you have them and he wants them back."

Danielle leapt over the treadmill's power cord. "He's on the move." By the time Millie hopped onto the treadmill rails and shut the machine off, Danielle was gone.

Cat sauntered over, dabbing at the beads of sweat with the towel draped around her neck. "Where's Danielle?"

"Chasing after Arvin, Tonya's suspected boyfriend."

"Is he a co-worker?" Cat's eyes scanned the room.

"No. He works down in recycling and waste management. I told Danielle maybe he was collecting trash."

"No way. The cleaning staff handles the above deck trash removal," Cat said.

"Which is why Danielle is trailing him. We better catch up with her." Millie gingerly opened the door leading into the hall and stuck her head around the corner. "Danielle?" she whispered.

Cat nudged Millie into the hall and shut the door.

A sharp *ping* echoed from the other end of the hall and Millie jumped. "What was that?"

"It's coming from down there." Cat and Millie kept to the side and slowly made their way to the other end of the hall. A shadowy figure darted around the dark corner.

"Uh." Millie took a quick step back and nearly tripped.

"It's Danielle," Cat said. "Hey!"

Danielle shook her head and pressed a finger to her lips.

"We gotta get down." Cat grabbed Millie's arm and pulled her down. They stayed there for several long moments before Danielle crawled across the floor and joined them.

"Well?" Millie asked. "Did you tail Arvin?"

"Yeah. I followed him into the hall and watched him try to open a bunch of the doors. I don't think he knew I was here until dummy me stubbed my toe on a doorjamb. Arvin heard it and took off. He was on his way out when you two showed up."

"Did he try to get into the spa employee breakroom?" Cat asked.

"Yep," Danielle nodded. "That's where he went first. The door was locked."

"I'm sure it is, especially after the break in," Millie pointed out.

"Which is why I brought this." Danielle flashed a small metal hook. "Remember this little gem the *Nutty Knitters* gave me? This oughta get us into the breakroom. After that, I think I can crack the code on the lockers' combination locks."

The women headed back down the hall and stopped in front of the breakroom door. Danielle slipped the metal hook inside the lock and wiggled it back and forth.

Click. "I think I got it." Danielle twisted the knob. "Shoot. Not yet."

A muffled scraping noise coming from the vicinity of the locker room made Millie jump. "Hurry. Someone is close by."

"I'm trying." Danielle gave her an exasperated look and held out the hook. "You wanna give it a go?"

"Sorry," Millie apologized. "Carry on."

"That's what I thought." Danielle squeezed one eye shut as she slid the hook into the lock a second time and slowly twisted it. *Pop.*

"Got it." She pushed the door open and slipped inside. Cat followed behind and Millie brought up the rear. "I still have an uneasy feeling something bad is about to happen. Let's hurry."

Danielle was a step ahead of her and already kneeling in front of the employee lockers. She gently pulled on the lock and waited for the faint click. Finally, she had all three combinations aligned. She removed the lock, opened the door and peered inside. "I...can't see a darn thing."

"This should help." Cat whipped out her cell phone and turned the light on.

"Much better. Thanks, Cat." Danielle carefully sifted through the contents. "There's nothing in here except work clothes and some deodorant. Next."

Danielle made quick work of opening the locker directly below it. It was filled with spa samples.

"There's nothing of value in these lockers."

"Maybe because they're easy to break into," Cat teased.

"Very funny." Danielle scooched sideways to the second row and opened the top locker. "Oh my gosh." She fell back on her butt, making a small choking sound.

"Ugh." Cat took a big whiff and almost dropped her phone trying to cover her mouth. "What *is* that?"

"What's what?" Millie, who was standing directly behind both of them, leaned forward. The overwhelming stench of vomit and sweat filled her nostrils. "Gross. What is it?"

"I don't know and I don't want to know," Danielle said.

"Me either." Cat pressed her hand over her mouth and nose. "Next."

"No. We gotta check it out. Step aside." Millie sucked in a quick breath of fresh air and stuck her hand inside the locker, pulling out a crusty gym towel. She tossed it over Danielle's head and it landed on the floor behind her.

Next, she pulled out a black polyester jacket. "This appears to be one of the spa worker's jackets." Millie held it at arm's length. "Shine your light on this Cat."

Cat's cell phone light caught a glimmer of something shiny. "There's a nametag. Tonya Rivera."

"This must be Tonya's locker." Millie set the jacket on the floor next to her and reached inside the locker a third time. Her fingers made contact with a plastic hook and a cloth strap. "I think I found something. It's a backpack."

Cat and Danielle crowded around as Millie unzipped the front compartment. It was empty.

Millie unzipped the second, also empty and then the third and largest compartment. It also appeared to be empty. She tipped it over and shook it. A small bottle of perfume and a tube of Chap Stick fell out.

"So much for a shocking discovery," Danielle said. "We might as well take a quick look inside the rest of the lockers while we're here."

Millie replaced the backpack first, followed by Tonya's work jacket. The crusty, smelly towel went in last.

Danielle finished her search of all of the lockers and slowly stood. "I guess we shouldn't be surprised. I'm sure Patterson and his men have searched every nook and cranny of the spa, looking for clues."

"We're not an iota closer to cracking this case." Millie zigzagged past the breakroom tables and stopped when she reached the door. "It looks like you're camping out on my sofa bed again."

"Although I appreciate the offer, I can't sleep on your sofa bed forever," Danielle said. "We need to set a trap."

"I say we sleep on it. It's been a long day and my brain is starting to get a little fuzzy," Millie said.

"Remember Millie's favorite saying…motive and opportunity," Cat said. "We have motive – pedaling prescription drugs. All we have to do is figure out the opportunity. It's looking more and more like Tonya had a partner in the prescription drug scheme. If we can figure out who her partner was, I think we'll have Danielle's intruder."

"And possibly Tonya's killer," Millie said. "If she was murdered. We still don't know if she accidentally overdosed."

"It doesn't make sense," Danielle insisted. "Why? And why plant a bottle in my jacket? No, I think someone is behind her overdose and trying to frame me. Add in her missing keycard, the surveillance camera in my cabin and last, but not least, the threatening note."

"All valid points." Millie rubbed a weary hand across her forehead. "Perhaps after a good night's rest, we'll be able to put our heads together and come up with a plan to catch the culprit."

"We need to get Annette involved," Cat said.

"That's a great idea. I'll send Annette a quick text, asking if we can meet in the galley tomorrow morning first thing. What time?"

"I can do seven," Cat said.

"Me too," Danielle said.

Millie tapped a message to Annette, who sent back a quick reply telling her that seven o'clock would be fine and she would have breakfast waiting for them.

"Sleuthing and cinnamon rolls," Millie smiled. "What better way to start the day?"

"Now let's get out of here before someone busts us." Cat eased the door open and stepped into the hall, running smack dab into the last person the trio hoped to see.

Chapter 17

"Hello, Cat." Patterson waited for Millie and Danielle to join her. "Millie, Danielle. Where's Annette?"

"Working," Millie said.

"Which is what the three of you should be doing. Instead, you're sticking your noses in where they don't belong. I could've saved you the trouble and told you I already searched the employee breakroom and lockers, if you made it that far."

"We did," Cat wrinkled her nose as she remembered the foul odor. "Unfortunately."

"How did you know we were here?" Millie asked.

Patterson pointed above their heads. "My men installed a surveillance camera this morning, after the spa manager reported a break in. I figured the culprit, or in this case, culprits would return, and I would catch them in the act. Little did I know it was you three." He sighed heavily. "Although I'm not sure why I'm surprised."

"This is the first time we've broken in," Danielle insisted, which was technically true since the last time they'd been inside the spa breakroom, the door had been unlocked.

"No harm, no foul," Millie said.

"Except for meddling in an ongoing murder investigation," Patterson pointed out.

"So Tonya was murdered," Danielle said.

"It's looking that way." Patterson lifted both hands. "Look, I could…I should write all three of you up for entering a restricted area."

"It wasn't restricted for me," Millie said. "I have unrestricted access ship-wide."

"You used your keycard to get in the breakroom?" Patterson's face turned bright red.

"No. I thought it best not to use my card," Millie mumbled.

"Because I could track it," Patterson sucked in a breath. "I'm sure you're aware that you're pushing the limits on company protocol. Regardless of your unrestricted access, you know where you should and shouldn't be."

Millie felt duly reprimanded and decided not to push her luck. Instead, she attempted to appease Patterson. "I'm sorry. We weren't trying to interfere in your investigation. As you pointed out, you already searched the breakroom."

"We were…uh, making sure you didn't miss anything," Cat said.

"How kind." Patterson turned to Danielle. "Unfortunately the video looped at the exact moment we spotted you chasing someone down this hall a short time before the three of you decided to break into the breakroom."

"I wasn't chasing. I was merely following a suspect."

"Who might that be?"

Danielle remembered Patterson's earlier accusations. "You tell me who's on the list of suspects and I'll tell you which one it is."

"You're treading on thin ice, Danielle."

"Fine." She crossed her arms. "It was Arvin Kurtz. As you know, Tonya and he were close. We're wondering if they were close as in lovers or close as in business associates."

"Business associates?" Patterson lifted a brow.

"You know what's going on. Tonya was signing for deliveries of prescription drugs, hence the *planted* pill bottle in my jacket." Danielle stressed the word planted. "Now that Tonya is dead, where are the drugs?"

"Or the money?" Millie added.

"You were searching for...cash or pills?" Patterson asked.

"Aren't you?" Cat blinked rapidly. "You're the professional."

Despite the seriousness of the conversation, Patterson cracked a smile. "I would like to think I am."

"We're also looking for a hoodie," Millie blurted out.

Danielle jabbed Millie with her elbow.

"A hoodie?"

"It's nothing," Millie mumbled.

"You fill me in on the hoodie and I'll let you three off the hook with a warning," Patterson bargained.

"We caught someone on video inside Danielle's cabin. The intruder was wearing a hoodie."

"I want to see the video," Patterson said.

"I think we could arrange an exchange," Danielle said. "You tell us what you know and we'll let you see the video; otherwise I'm not inclined to show it to you."

Patterson's expression grew stormy. He clamped onto Danielle's arm and began escorting her toward the exit.

"What are you doing?" Danielle gasped.

"I'm taking you to the holding cell to give you time to work on an attitude adjustment, especially towards me."

"You can't do that." Danielle attempted to jerk her arm from Patterson's grasp, but he kept a vice grip hold, refusing to let go.

Millie and Cat exchanged a worried glance and hurried after them.

"I can and I will." Patterson didn't slow until they reached the bank of elevators near the spa entrance. He jabbed the down button and waited for the doors to open.

Thankfully, there was no one inside and he pulled her in.

For a split second, Millie thought about taking the stairs, but took one look at Patterson's unreadable expression and quickly joined them.

Cat followed her in and the four of them rode to deck two in silence. The doors opened and Danielle and Patterson stepped into the hall.

Despite the ominous look, Millie knew she needed to try to rescue Danielle. "Danielle is under a lot of stress right now. Her roommate just died, someone is spying on her and leaving her threatening notes. Could you cut her a little slack?"

Her plea was met with stony silence, but she wasn't ready to give up. "I'll be responsible for her," Millie promised.

"Or I will," Cat chimed in. "Those cells are for bad people and Danielle is not one of them. They're dark and creepy."

"I've made up my mind." Patterson stopped in front of the holding cell, swiped his keycard and then punched in the access code.

The door let out a low ominous creak, as it swung open.

Danielle cast Millie a look of utter misery, but kept silent as Patterson escorted her inside. The door shut behind them and Millie felt like bursting into tears. "This is terrible."

Cat stared at the door. "I feel responsible."

"Me too. We should've known after Camille told us about the break in and someone ransacking the place that Patterson would install cameras."

"Yeah, we're real slick sleuthers," Cat said gloomily.

Patterson emerged moments later. "Don't even think about letting her out or else I will write you up. All three of you."

"Are you going to write Danielle up?" Millie thought of Danielle's letter of resignation. A write up...and a lock up might be the icing on the cake. The thought left a queasy feeling in the pit of her stomach.

"No. I'm giving Danielle the opportunity to reflect on her attitude and maybe, just maybe, by tomorrow morning, she'll see I'm here to help her. For now, she's out of trouble and I can keep an eye on her." Patterson wagged his finger in warning. "I can do the same to you, too, so you better be on your best behavior."

"Oh, I will," Cat's head bobbed up and down. "I'm going straight to my cabin and going to bed."

"Can I at least bring Danielle a change of clothes?" Although a small sink and toilet were inside the holding cell, along with a lumpy mattress and a couple of thin blankets, there wasn't much else.

"You can bring them to my office and I'll make sure she gets them." Patterson answered Millie's next question before she could ask. "I'll let her out first thing in the morning. It will be up to her whether she wants to tell Andy where she spent the night."

Patterson turned on his heel and marched across the hall to his office. He stepped inside and closed the door behind him.

"I still can't believe it." Millie shook her head. "I can't believe Patterson stuck Danielle in the holding cell."

"She was a little belligerent towards him." Cat fell into step with Millie. "Are you going to bring her some stuff?"

"Yeah. She has her cell phone, although cell service doesn't work inside the holding area. I could bring her a snack, some clothes, a toothbrush, the essentials to get her through the night."

"You're a good friend, Millie, even when we get into a pinch," Cat complimented.

"Thanks. So are you, Cat." Millie told her friend good-bye and continued walking to the other end of the ship where Danielle's cabin was located.

When she stepped inside, tears burned the back of her eyes at the thought of her friend locked up and all alone.

Millie found the backpack Danielle had left earlier and filled it with things she thought she could use, careful to avoid staring at the surveillance cameras as she worked.

She returned to Patterson's office. His expression was as gloomy as Millie's. "I'm sorry."

"I know and I'm sure Danielle is sorry, too." Patterson leaned back in his chair. "That woman has a stubborn streak a mile long." He opened his mouth to say something and then stopped.

"What?" Millie asked. "What were you going to say?"

"Nothing. I...you'll find out soon enough."

"I'm not leaving until you tell me."

"It's about Brody and Danielle. You'll have to ask Danielle."

Millie plopped down in a chair. "They're getting married?"

She could tell from the look on Patterson's face that wasn't it.

"Having a baby and getting married?" *Still not right.*

Finally, it dawned on her and Millie pressed a hand to her chest. "They broke up."

"Brody just left. He asked me to transfer him back to the night shift. I had no idea. No wonder Danielle was cranky."

"Cranky…cranky? She's heartbroken and now she's locked up in the holding cell." Millie sprang to her feet. "Don't you think that's punishment enough? Maybe you should let her out."

"I can't. She'll wonder why and I promised Brody I wouldn't say anything. I shouldn't have told you." Patterson pushed Danielle's backpack toward Millie. "I think you should take these to her, make sure she's all right."

"I would tell you I think you overreacted...unintentionally, of course, but I think you already know that." Millie snatched the backpack off the desk. "I also think you need sensitivity training toward the opposite sex."

She stopped short of giving him a piece of her mind. Judging by the guilty look on his face, he was feeling bad enough. Not as bad as Danielle, but still. "I'll talk to Danielle and won't let on I know about the break up."

Millie slipped out of his office and crossed the hall. She swiped her card, punched in the access code and waited for the *click*.

"Danielle?" Millie slowly eased the door open. Her heart sank at the sight of her young friend, sprawled out on the narrow bunk, an arm flung across her face. "I brought you some things."

"Thanks, Millie. You can leave them on the floor."

Millie approached the bunk and knelt down next to it. "I think Patterson is regretting his decision."

"He should be. I'm not a criminal. Sure, I mouthed off a little, but he's acting like I committed a crime."

Millie couldn't disagree, although she could also see Patterson's side, how he was irritated and aggravated by their interfering. "I see both sides."

"I'm fine," Danielle sighed. "Thanks for bringing me my stuff. Patterson said I'll be out first thing tomorrow morning." She lifted her arm and stared at Millie. "At least I don't have to worry about the intruder following me in here."

Despite the seriousness of the situation, Millie laughed. "True. Unless Patterson catches him and throws him in here, too."

"Right?" Danielle smiled.

"I'm always here for you...you know that, right?"

"I do. Thanks, Millie."

"For getting you thrown into the slammer?"

"No, for being my friend."

"I love you," Millie said.

"I love you, too."

The women chatted for a few more minutes, until Millie was certain Danielle would be all right. "I better get going. Nic will be wondering what happened to me."

Danielle shifted to a sitting position. "So we're still on to meet Annette in the galley at seven tomorrow morning?"

"Yes. We're still on."

"Great. See you then."

Millie gave Danielle a gentle hug and then made her way out of the holding cell. Her heart felt as cold as the sound of the door closing behind her. She said a small prayer for her friend as she slowly made her way home.

The guilt over going home to a man she loved, to a pup who brightened her day and a home she adored, knowing Danielle was all alone and locked up, was almost unbearable.

Nic was already in the apartment when Millie arrived. "You look like you lost your best friend."

"Close." Millie slumped into an empty chair and kicked her shoes off. "Patterson locked Danielle in the holding cell for the night."

"You're kidding." Nic's eyes grew wide. "What happened...wait a minute. What did you do this time?"

"Why does it always have to be my fault?"

"So it wasn't you?"

"It was me." Millie's shoulders sagged. "Danielle, Cat and I decided to have a look around the spa breakroom after hours. Patterson caught us, Danielle gave him a little lip and he locked her up."

"Millie Armati..."

"I know, I know." Millie lifted a hand. "Patterson already lectured all of us. Danielle will be out first thing in the morning. I dropped some things off for her and stayed long enough to make sure she'll be okay." She changed the subject. "Let's talk about more pleasant things."

"I agree." A slow smile spread across Nic's face. "I have a great surprise in store for our date day."

Chapter 18

Millie's mind drew a blank. "Date day?"

"Our day off in St. Kitts. You forgot already?"

"I don't even know what day of the week it is."

"It's Monday. We left St. Martin a few hours ago. We have a sea day tomorrow and then Wednesday we'll be in St. Kitts."

"Now I remember. So what's the surprise?" Millie asked.

"If I told you, it wouldn't be a surprise. You'll have to wait and see."

Millie wasn't a huge fan of surprises…except if Nic was planning them. She remembered their romantic picnic on a secluded beach where he proposed, how he surprised her with their dream honeymoon at the *Grand Bay Beach Club*.

"I'm sure it will be wonderful." Millie stifled a yawn. "I'm whupped and I have to be up early for a meeting in the galley with Annette."

Nic followed his wife up the stairs. "Are you taking up cooking and plan to whip up some fabulous homemade meals?"

Millie shot her husband a quick glance. "Would you like me to make a home cooked meal?" Since joining the Siren of the Seas, she had only dabbled in cooking when she was in the galley with Annette, brainstorming over the latest mystery.

"It might be nice once in a while, but I know you're as busy as I am."

"You're right. It would be nice to cook something homemade every once in a while." Although their apartment kitchen was on the small side, it was equipped with everything necessary to whip up a gourmet dinner or some good, old-fashioned comfort food. "What sounds good to you?"

"You really want to make me something?"

"Of course. I would love to."

"Let me think about it."

The couple took turns getting ready for bed and Scout, who was already in bed, crept to the center after Millie climbed in.

She patted his head. "Do you miss Danielle?" she cooed.

Scout let out a faint yip, before spinning in a circle to find a comfortable spot and flopping down. "Hopefully, we can figure out who's stalking her and sneaking into her cabin."

"She's welcome to stay here as long as it takes," Nic said.

"Thanks. I appreciate that."

Millie's heart was heavy as they prayed for Danielle, for their families and for a smooth sea day.

She slept fitfully, tossing and turning all night. Every time she woke, her mind was on Danielle.

Nic was still asleep the next morning when she snuck into the bathroom to get ready. After finishing, Millie tiptoed across the bedroom and opened the door. Scout, excited to be up early, began barking.

"Shhh. Be quiet."

It was too late. "You're up already?" Nic asked his voice heavy with sleep.

"Yes. I'm worried about Danielle. I want to check on her before meeting Annette in the galley."

"I might as well get up, too." Nic stumbled to the bathroom.

"I'm sorry. I didn't mean to wake you."

"It's okay. I didn't sleep well, either."

"You're worried about Danielle, too?"

"No. I was dreaming about the delicious feast you're going to make me."

"Do you have a feast in mind?"

Nic murmured something incoherent and disappeared inside the bathroom while Millie followed Scout downstairs. She let him out and started a pot of strong coffee, certain she was facing another long day.

Nic joined her a short time later. "In my half-awake state of mind, I thought you mentioned checking on Danielle."

"I did and I am."

"You're a wonderful friend and a wonderful wife." Nic embraced his wife, wrapping both arms around her before placing a gentle kiss on top of her head. "I can't wait to find out if you're a wonderful cook."

Millie pulled back. "What if I'm not a wonderful cook? What if I'm an awful, horrible can't-boil-water cook?"

"Then it's a good thing you're an assistant cruise director and not a sous chef," her husband teased.

"Dork." Millie playfully swatted at her husband before pouring coffee in a to-go Thermos. "Annette made the most amazing pumpkin crunch cake."

"I love pumpkin. Maybe you can practice your baking skills and make me one."

"That's what I'll do." She handed him the Thermos and gave him a quick kiss before breezing out of the apartment.

Her mood sobered by the time she reached the holding cell. Millie rapped lightly before using her keycard and entering the code to open the door. "Danielle?" She stuck her head inside. The dim overhead light was on.

"I'm up." Danielle struggled to a sitting position. "This has to be the most uncomfortable bunk on the ship. It's more like a cot."

"Three hots and a cot," Millie joked.

"I don't need three hots and a cot. I need my own bed and some decent food." Danielle pressed a hand to her back and slowly stood. "Are you here to spring me or do I have to wait for Patterson?"

Millie hadn't thought that far ahead. "I'm here to check on you." She glanced at her watch. "Patterson should be along shortly. Let me give him a call on the radio."

She stepped into the hall and reached for her radio before noticing the security office light was on, so she figured she'd try there first.

Patterson was in his office. He looked up when Millie stepped inside. "You're up early."

"I was worried about Danielle and decided to come down to check on her. You're going to let her out soon, right?"

"Yes. I was finishing up some paperwork on Tonya's investigation." Patterson pushed his chair back and stood.

Millie noticed the dark circles under his eyes. "You didn't sleep well, either."

"Nope."

"Because you felt guilty about Danielle, but couldn't go back on your decision," Millie guessed.

"Something like that. I would like a word with her alone," Patterson said.

"Of course. I'll hang out here." Millie settled into a nearby seat to wait.

Patterson returned to his office a short time later. Danielle strolled in behind him. "Danielle showed me the video of the intruder inside her cabin. I take this matter very seriously and have her permission to search her cabin again."

"You're wasting your time," Millie said. "You've searched the cabin, we've searched the cabin. It's clean."

"Yes, but whoever is breaking in may be after something," Patterson said. "It's worth having another look around."

Danielle slung the backpack over her shoulder. "I'm ready to blow this joint."

"I can't blame you." Millie popped out of her chair and opened the office door. She waited until they were a safe distance away from Patterson's office before speaking.

"Do you still want to meet with us in the galley?" Millie asked.

"Of course, now more than ever. Whoever this is, is most likely not only responsible for Tonya's overdose…"

Millie abruptly stopped. "Patterson confirmed that she died of an overdose?"

"Yes. Traces of the same drug, an opioid, were found inside the pill bottle that was in my work jacket."

When Danielle and Millie reached the galley, Cat, Annette and Amit were already waiting. "Sorry if we're late. We got a little hung up down in Patterson's office."

"Cat told me what happened." Annette made her way to Danielle's side, a concerned expression on her face. "I can't believe Patterson locked you in the holding cell."

"I deserved to be locked up," Danielle said. "I was mouthing off and he called me out, but thanks for the backup. I told Millie the investigators determined the cause of Tonya's death was a drug overdose. The investigators haven't ruled out suicide, accidental overdose or homicide."

"Let's go over the list of suspects, so I can get up to speed," Annette said.

"I spent the night working on the list." Danielle reached inside her backpack and pulled out a pad of yellow paper and a pen. "First is Arvin Kurtz. Tonya insisted they weren't an item even though they spent a lot of time together."

"Arvin and Tonya both worked on board the Marquise of the Seas before transferring to the Siren of the Seas," Millie said.

"And Arvin was in the gym last night," Cat added.

"Definitely a suspect," Annette agreed. "Who else?"

"Camille Bessette, the spa manager. She put Tonya in charge of picking up and signing for the spa packages," Danielle said.

"And according to Joy, the receptionist, Tonya and Camille were also friends," Millie said.

"Just those two," Danielle tapped the top of her notepad. "It should be easy to narrow it down."

"There's one more." Millie rubbed her forehead. She hadn't considered this person before, but the more she thought about it, the more she suspected he might be involved. "What about Stephen Chow?"

"Chow the acupuncturist?" Danielle asked. "Why would he be a suspect?"

"Sharky told me Tonya was also signing for deliveries for Stephen Chow. What if Chow was bringing in prescription drugs and then he and Tonya were selling them?"

"Chow can't prescribe prescription drugs," Annette said. "The only one who can do that is Doc Gundervan."

"Maybe Joe Gundervan is the dealer," Cat said.

Millie's mouth dropped open, shocked by Cat's statement. "Do you honestly believe he could be involved in pedaling prescription drugs?"

"Maybe," Cat shifted her feet. "I wouldn't put anything past him at this point."

Millie placed a gentle hand on her shoulder. "Are you all right?"

Cat quickly looked down, but not before Millie noticed unshed tears threatening to spill over. "What's wrong?"

Instead of answering, Cat broke free from Millie's grasp and ran from the room.

Chapter 19

Annette shook her head. "I guess Cat and Gundervan hit the skids."

"It must be going around," Danielle muttered.

"I'll go after her." Millie hurried out of the galley and into the empty corridor. Certain that Cat was hiding out in the store, she power-walked to the store and began pounding on the door. She noticed a flicker of movement and caught a glimpse of Cat's bright pink jacket.

"Let me in," Millie hollered.

When Cat didn't open the door, Millie started pounding harder, hard enough to make the glass rattle.

It worked. Cat reluctantly opened the door and motioned her friend inside. "Misery doesn't love company."

"I'm not company. I'm your friend. Annette, Danielle, Amit...we're your friends and we're concerned."

"It's nothing."

"No, it's something. What happened?"

"Joe and I made plans for another date day tomorrow in St. Kitts, to hike up Mount Liamuiga after he cancelled last time. I was so excited; I even bought a pair of hiking boots in Miami. Do you know how hard it is to find a pair of hiking boots in Florida?"

Cat didn't wait for Millie to answer. "Last night after Patterson busted us, I ran down to the medical clinic to say 'hi' to Joe since the medical clinic had closed."

Millie interrupted. "You caught him with Rachel."

"No. He cancelled our date again. I asked if it had anything to do with Rachel. He got defensive and told me I was acting like a jealous girlfriend. I told him he was acting like a man torn between two lovers and then I stormed out."

"I'm sorry, Cat. Maybe it has nothing to do with Rachel. You should have given him a chance to explain."

"You're right. I guess I should have." Cat's lower lip trembled. "I think he's playing games and stringing me along."

"Danielle and Brody broke up, too," Millie said. "Although we're not supposed to know that."

"Oh no. I thought they were such a cute couple. Poor Danielle. She's had it rough these past few days."

"No kidding, that's why we've got to figure out who is breaking into her cabin and who left a threatening note."

"My minor love life troubles are nothing compared to Danielle's problems," Cat said. "Don't worry about me. I'll be fine. I need to start work early today anyways. It's our gold-by-the-inch sale day and we're gonna be slammed."

Millie had a sudden thought. "Do you still have tomorrow off?"

"Yes. Maybe I'll stay in bed and sleep all day," Cat said miserably.

"Not a chance. Nic has something planned for us tomorrow, but he has to be back early in the afternoon and I want to do some shopping in Basseterre, the town right near the port." Millie squeezed her friend's hand. "Will you go shopping with me?"

Cat shook her head. "I don't want to ruin your date day."

"You won't be. Nic will be back on board the ship and I need a shopping buddy," Millie said. "I insist."

"Okay." Cat offered Millie a watery smile. "It would take my mind off my troubles, at least for a little while."

"Perfect. I'll let you know later what time to meet me on the dock." She gave Cat a quick hug. "I better get back to the galley. Are you sure you're okay?"

"I'm fine. Maybe Joe and I need some time apart to cool off," Cat wisely said.

"I agree." Millie told her friend good-bye and then returned to the galley where Danielle, Annette and Amit were waiting.

"Well?" Annette asked.

"Gundervan and Cat got into another argument." Millie briefly explained what happened.

"Men are jerks," Danielle glanced at Amit. "Except for you, Amit. You're a cool dude."

"Thanks, Miss Danielle. That's why I stay away from women," Amit said.

"So what's the plan?" Danielle asked.

"We need to set up some sort of sting," Millie said.

"I have an idea. It's only in the planning stages," Annette said. "It might take me a little time to work out all of the details. Cooking always helps clear my mind."

"Speaking of cooking, I told Nic I would make a homemade dish for him. I mentioned your pumpkin crunch cake and he sounded excited."

"My pumpkin crunch cake? I'll get you the recipe." Annette held up a finger. "Be right back." She stepped into the dry pantry and returned with a small recipe box. "I store most of my recipes on the computer, but keep my handy dandy recipe box nearby as a backup."

She began thumbing through the index cards. "Here it is."

Millie plucked her cell phone from her pocket and snapped a picture. "I think I can handle making this."

"I call it *Pumpkin Crunch Cake Kauai Style*. A friend of mine, who lives in Hawaii, shared it with me."

"Where will I get all of these ingredients?" Millie frowned as she studied the list.

"Right here in my kitchen. If you want to stop by in your free time and grab what you need, my kitchen is your kitchen."

"Thanks, Annette. You're the best."

Danielle and Millie told Annette and Amit goodbye and stepped into the corridor. "I want to stop by my cabin to take a shower and drop my stuff off."

"I'll go with you."

The women swung by Danielle's cabin to drop her things off and hung around long enough for her to take a shower before heading to Andy's office.

Andy was already there, along with several other staff members. "Glad you could make it."

"We had a busy morning," Danielle said.

"You could say that," Millie mumbled.

"Let's get down to business. Today is the official kickoff of the fall festivities. We're opening the haunted house, creating Halloween costumes with the kids, followed by trick or treating later this evening."

"Trick or treating? How will you do that?" Millie interrupted.

"Passenger volunteers." Andy went on to explain his brilliant idea of passing out candy and stickers to passengers who wanted to participate. They would place the sticker on their cabin door, so the children would know which passengers/cabins were participating.

"That is a good idea," Millie turned to Danielle. "It sounds as if you're going to be one busy lady."

"You're not off the hook," Andy warned. "We have adult activities planned, too." He handed Millie her daily schedule.

"A donut dash, hay-z maze." She looked up. "We have hay on board the ship?"

"Yes, although I was only able to get a couple of bales. I borrowed some of our event drapery to create the maze. The maintenance guys are setting it up in the conference room today."

"Ah." Millie lifted a brow. "The conference room is the perfect spot since the place sits empty most of the time." She continued studying the list of events. It ended with a champagne toast and black and orange balloon drop in the atrium. "You oughta knock this one out of the park, Andy."

"That's my plan. Today is our day to shine. It's make it or break it."

"Why not wait until the last sea day?" one of the staff members asked.

"Passengers are busy worrying about packing, settling their sail and sign bills and enjoying their last day of fun in the sun. Today is our only other sea day since we'll be in St. Kitts tomorrow and Grand Turk the following day."

Andy answered a few more questions as the staff grabbed a copy of their work schedules and headed out.

Millie was the last to leave and Andy stopped her. "Hey, Millie. Hang on."

She waited until they were alone. "What's up?"

"How's Danielle? I heard Brody and she broke up."

"She seems to be taking it all right, although it's hard to tell with Danielle."

"Patterson is still working on figuring out what happened to her cabin mate."

"She died of a drug overdose," Millie said. "From what I heard, he's still not sure if it was accidental."

"That's tough," Andy said. "So you like my fall festivities?"

"Yes, they're great. You have quite an imagination. I am curious about one thing…what did you do with the stinky scarecrows?"

"I'm using them as props near the entrance to the maze."

Millie wrinkled her nose. "They smell."

"Nope. Not anymore."

"Are you sure?"

"I'm positive. Smell for yourself." Millie followed Andy out of the office and to the costume storage area.

She leaned in, took a big whiff of the nearest scarecrow and made a gagging noise. "I can still smell it."

"No way." Andy lifted the scarecrow's straw arm and sniffed. "You're imagining it."

"No, I'm not," Millie insisted. "You can't put these out in public. They smell awful."

"I *am* going to put them out."

"Fine. Suit yourself. Don't say I didn't warn you."

"You seriously think the scarecrows smell?" Andy asked.

"I do." Millie tilted her head and studied her boss. "Let's place a friendly wager."

"Why not? You're going to lose. I can't smell anything."

"Okay." Millie folded her arms; remembering her vow to get even with her boss for making her wear the witch costume. "Tell you what…if even one passenger comments about the odor, then *you* get to wear the witch costume to greet guests returning to the ship in St. Kitts."

"I…that's cruel and unusual punishment," Andy said.

"Oh really? You didn't seem to think so when you forced me to wear it to the movie marathon the other day."

Andy knew Millie had him. "Fine. If even one person comments about a bad smell, I'll wear the witch's hat and cape."

"And the nose, don't forget the nose," Millie said.

"And the nose, but that's where I draw the line. The pointed witch shoes will never fit me."

Millie smiled triumphantly as she held out her hand. "It's not a deal until we shake."

Andy gave Millie's hand a quick shake. "Now get to work before I make you put it on again today."

"Aye, aye." She gave her boss a mock salute and sauntered out of the theater. Today was shaping up to be a great day, after all.

The rest of the day passed in a blur as Millie dashed from one event to the next. She barely had enough time to grab a sandwich for lunch before starting the afternoon activities.

She ran into Danielle once, in passing and she wore the same harried expression as Millie.

The evening's headliner was a magic show, followed by the hay-z maze. Millie planned to stop by the maze earlier in the day to check it out, but never found the time.

She arrived promptly at seven o'clock, fifteen minutes before the maze was scheduled to open.

Impressed by Andy's creativity, Millie wandered through the maze, where each corner was decorated in a fall theme. There were pumpkins and twinkling leaf lights, bushels of apples and baskets of pinecones. Along the top of each section was a string of berry garland.

"Well?" Andy snuck up behind her. "How did I do?"

"It's impressive," Millie said. "You really outdid yourself."

"Did you see the scarecrows?"

"No."

"Follow me." Andy led her through the maze and back to the entrance.

Standing sentinel on each side were the scarecrows. Millie caught a whiff of the rancid odor. "Yuck."

"You still smell it?"

"Yup," Millie nodded. "If possible, it's even stronger now."

"You're imagining things."

"We'll see."

Millie hung out near the entrance to greet the passengers who wandered in. She briefly explained how the maze worked. "When you reach the end, it opens to the main corridor. Follow the signs one deck down where the captain is hosting a champagne toast and balloon drop later this evening."

"What time is the balloon drop?"

"At ten," Millie said. "Before the toast and balloon drop, there will be live music and free appetizers."

The guests were excited about the maze and the first group passed through, walking right past the scarecrows.

"See?" Andy gloated. "You were wrong and I was right. Now you get to wear the witch costume again on departure day."

"The night is still young," Millie said. "Just wait." She greeted another large group and after explaining the maze, the passengers headed toward the entrance.

The first two walked through, followed by a trio of passengers, two women and a man. They abruptly stopped in front of the scarecrows.

Chapter 20

"Here we go," Millie whispered as she elbowed her boss.

Andy ignored the jab.

"What is that awful smell?" A woman's voice rang out and Millie choked back a laugh.

The other woman leaned in and sniffed the scarecrow. "This scarecrow smells like rotting fish."

"No, it smells like sewer gas."

The man who was with them took a whiff. "More like decaying flesh."

The trio gave the offensive scarecrows a wide berth and hurried inside the maze.

Millie couldn't help it. She doubled over in gales of laughter as visions of Andy wearing her witch's costume filled her head.

Andy plucked his radio from his belt. "Maintenance to the conference room ASAP."

Two of the maintenance crewmembers arrived moments later and Andy explained he needed the scarecrows moved to a storage room, away from the guest area.

"These things reek," one of them said.

Millie smiled triumphantly as the maintenance workers loaded the offensive duo onto handcarts and wheeled them out of the room. "You are going to look so *cute* in my witch's costume."

"Very funny. I think you sprayed them with something before I got here."

"I did not," Millie said indignantly. "Don't be a sore loser. I won the bet fair and square."

A glum Andy departed a short time later and the smile never left Millie's face the entire evening.

At ten on the dot, Nic made an appearance in the atrium for the champagne toast and balloon drop.

During his brief speech, he thanked the passengers for sailing on board the Siren of the Seas.

Finally, it was time for Millie to head home. Nic joined her a short time later, reminding her that tomorrow they would be stopping in St. Kitts and it was their day off. As Millie drifted off to sleep, she wondered what Nic had in store for them.

Early the next morning, Millie bounced out of bed, excited for their date day. Her excitement was contagious and Nic willingly forfeited the precious extra minutes of sleep to join his wife downstairs for a leisurely breakfast.

"What should I bring for our date day?" Millie reached for a donut hole.

"I would wear some old clothes and bring along a change of clothes. You'll need sunglasses, some sunscreen and a beach towel." Nic paused. "That should about do it."

"Old clothes?" Millie wrinkled her nose.

"Yes." Nic noted the panicked look on his wife's face. "Don't worry. It will be fun. I left a backpack on the bed. My things are already packed."

She opened her mouth to reply and quickly closed it. Nic had never let her down. She trusted him that they would have a good time. "I better go pack my stuff."

Millie trudged up the stairs and into the bedroom. She rummaged through her dresser drawer until she found an old pair of khaki shorts and faded t-shirt. She pulled them on before placing a clean set of clothes, a beach towel and sunscreen inside, and carried the backpack down the steps. "I'm ready."

"Don't look so excited," Nic teased. "I'll have you know we're embarking on the most popular St. Kitts island adventure, and I can assure you we will enjoy every minute of it. It may be some time before we're able to explore the island again."

"Don't remind me," Millie said glumly.

"And don't be a party pooper." Nic took the backpack from his wife and slung it over his shoulder.

The couple was one of the first in line at the gangway. They stepped off the ship and Nic pointed to a woman who was holding a sign, *St. Kitts Dune Buggy.* "Over there."

"This isn't a ship excursion?" Millie asked.

"No. I found them while I was doing some research. The company gets glowing reviews. Captain Vitale took the dune buggy tour about a month ago and loved it."

The woman, Patty, led them to a waiting van and they climbed in. Several other cruise ship passengers joined the couple. Because Millie and Nic were dressed in street clothes, she hoped the passengers wouldn't recognize them. One of the women gave Millie an odd look, but never commented.

During the ride, Patty pointed out various landmarks along the way. "In 1493, Christopher Columbus was allegedly so smitten with the volcanic island of St. Kitts; he named it after St. Christopher, the patron saint of travelers."

"Since its discovery, St. Christopher, which was later shortened to St. Kitts by British sailors, has been fought over by the British and French."

Patty also told them that pirates, including the notorious William "Captain" Kidd who was marooned on Nevis after his crew mutinied, enjoyed lucrative careers in Basseterre Harbor.

St. Kitts and sister isle, Nevis, were part of the British Empire until 1967, earning semi-independent status when they were named associated states of Great Britain. In 1983, St. Kitts and Nevis became an independent, two-island nation with a parliamentary government headed by a prime minister.

"What do St. Kitts' islanders do in their free time?" a passenger asked.

"Good question," Patty replied. "Golfing is a popular pastime, along with snorkeling and scuba diving. While British holdovers such as cricket and driving on the left side of the road remain, the St. Kitts' residents nicknamed 'Kittitians' are extremely proud of their history and how far they've come on their own."

Their ride ended in an unpaved parking lot. Lining the lot was a row of black and white four-wheel drive buggies.

Mel and Tack, the tour guides, instructed the group on how to drive the buggies and then assigned the participants to their respective buggies.

Nic climbed behind the wheel and Millie reluctantly joined him in the passenger seat. "Have you ever driven a dune buggy before?"

"No." Nic was grinning from ear-to-ear. "It can't be that hard." He turned the engine on and shifted into low gear.

The guides let the drivers practice in the parking lot before lining them up to begin the tour.

Tack made his way along the line of buggies. When he reached theirs, he handed Millie a plastic bag.

"What's this?"

"Bottled waters, bandanas and goggles."

"Bandanas and goggles?" Millie peeked inside the bag.

"The roads...they are very dusty," Tack explained. "You'll want to tie the bandana across your face, and wear the goggles to keep the dirt out of your eyes. Don't worry, after we're done, we'll stop at the beach to rinse off."

Millie shot her husband a questioning look. "Did Captain Vitale tell you we would get dirty?"

"Yes, but like Tack pointed out...we'll have time to wash off."

"Huh." Millie handed her husband a bandana and a pair of goggles. She smoothed the bandana across her face and tied it in the back before wiggling the goggles in place.

"Millie."

"What?"

Nic snapped a picture of his wife. "You look adorable."

"Give me that." Millie snatched the phone from his hand and took a picture of him. "You better hang onto this picture, because I don't think you'll ever catch me doing this again."

Nic laughed at his wife's grumbling. "Give it a chance, Millie. It will be fun."

She didn't have time to answer. Tack climbed into the lead dune buggy and Millie and Nic, who were smack dab in the middle of the pack, were off.

Millie's heart leapt into her chest, as the buggies hit the road and veered into the left lane. She quickly realized the traffic flow was opposite of what she was accustomed to and all of the buggies, including their guides, were driving on the left hand side.

The buggies zipped along the main road, which ran along the shoreline before turning onto an interior road. Large plumes of dust filled the air and Millie was thankful for the goggles and bandana. Several times, she ran her finger across the lenses to clear the dust.

The interior road twisted and turned. When they hit the straightaways, the buggies picked up speed, hitting several bumps hard enough for Millie to bounce out of her seat, despite her seatbelt. She squeezed her eyes shut and prayed for God's protection.

The buggy swerved and her eyes flew open.

"Sorry," Nic apologized. "I thought I saw something in the road.

Millie cast her husband a sideways glance, noting the expression of pure joy on his face. Admittedly the buggy ride was fun and although it was blazing hot, the roof kept the sun from beating directly down on them.

Beads of sweat trickled down her forehead and she longed for a drink of water, but didn't dare take the bandana off.

When Millie was certain she couldn't stand another gust of gray dust, they abruptly stopped.

She flipped the goggles up and the bandana down. Millie guzzled her bottle of water and then followed Nic and the others up a narrow dirt path to the top of a steep hill. The hilltop offered sweeping views of the island, as far as the eye could see.

Off in the distance was Mount Liamuiga. Tack told them Mount Liamuiga was an almost four thousand-foot stratovolcano, a volcano built up of alternate layers of lava and ash.

Millie and Nic took a few selfies and when she glanced at the pictures, she couldn't help but laugh at the layer of dirt coating her face, a stark contrast to the white circles around her eyes where the goggles protected them.

"Don't we look a sight?" Nic said.

"We look like dirty bank robbers wearing these bandannas," Millie joked. "I think we should print a copy and frame it."

"I agree." Nic was still smiling as he tugged his bandanna back over his face and adjusted his goggles.

The guides made several more stops before reaching the paved main road.

Millie hastily removed the dusty bandana and gulped in the fresh, clean air as they sped along the road.

The group stopped for a quick bathroom break, followed by several more miles of trail and road. Finally, the buggies were back where they started.

Patty, the driver, was waiting for them. "Did you have fun?"

All unanimously agreed they enjoyed their beach buggy excursion. Even Millie had to admit it was a picturesque ride, despite the dust and dirt. Nic gave Tack and Mel each a generous cash tip before climbing inside the van for the return trip.

Their drop off was a beach area, within walking distance of the ship. Millie and Nic opted to rinse off in the shower area and dry off with their beach towels.

"I'm sorry, Millie. It's time for me to return to the ship. Captain Vitale, Donovan and I have another conference call with corporate."

"That's okay. Cat is going to meet me on the dock. We plan to wander around Basseterre and do a little shopping."

"Thanks again for the date day." Nic gave his wife a quick kiss before climbing the gangway and disappearing from sight. After he was gone, Millie texted Cat to let her know she was waiting for her on the dock.

Cat arrived a short time later. She took one look at Millie and started laughing. "Oh my gosh. What in the world happened to you?"

"Nic surprised me with a dune buggy excursion. It included driving up and down a bunch of dusty trails."

"Better you than me," Cat joked. "Are you sure you still want to go shopping?"

"Yes, unless you're too embarrassed to be seen with me."

"Not at all." Cat linked arms with Millie. "I've been itching to get off the ship all day."

The women meandered in and out of the souvenir shops. Millie purchased a handcrafted piece of pottery from one of the vendors while Cat found a pair of earrings she insisted she couldn't live without.

They each sampled a coconut dumpling, touted as a St. Kitt's national dish. The women hit every touristy street and finally, it was time to head back to the ship.

"Thanks for hanging out with me, Cat." Millie gazed up at the clear blue skies. "I'm going to miss the islands."

"Me, too. I am excited for an overseas adventure, though. We'll be back before you know it."

"I hope so." Up ahead, Millie noticed a long line of people making the trek along the main thoroughfare back toward the ship. "It's going to take forever to get back on board the ship."

"I almost got caught up in that mess a couple of weeks ago when I got off the ship to pick up a few things. I know a shortcut. Follow me." Cat grabbed Millie's hand and pulled her onto a side street.

It appeared to be more of a locals' area, with a bank on the far corner and a small grocery store across the street. In between were several other small shops.

"This is much better," Millie said.

"Right? This street runs parallel to the main street and ends directly across from the port. The only difference is a lot less people."

A movement up ahead caught Millie's attention. It was a person who was moving at a fast clip. The person darted inside a building.

When they passed by the building, Millie casually glanced inside and abruptly stopped when she recognized the person standing at the counter.

Chapter 21

Millie slowed. "Do you see what I see?"

"Yes. It's a store."

"No. Do you see the person inside, standing at the counter?"

Cat peered through the glass. "Yes. Yes, I sure do."

"What is this place?" Millie tilted her head back and stared at the sign along the front of the building. *Port Square Pharmacy*. "We need to remember the name. Port Square Pharmacy."

"Let's hang out over there and see what happens." Cat pointed to the building next door.

The women darted to the doorway. Millie stuck her head around the corner and watched as the ship's employee exited the pharmacy a short time later, carrying a small white package.

"Let's go." Millie sprang from the alley and began following the person.

Cat ran to keep up. "What are we going to do...tackle her?"

"No. I was thinking more along the lines of beating her back to the ship," Millie said breathlessly.

"This isn't going to work," Cat gasped. "We need a stall tactic."

Millie's mind raced as she ran. "I think I have an idea. Hold up."

The women abruptly stopped. Millie reached into her pocket and pulled out her cell phone. She dialed the ship's main number and asked to be transferred to the gangway security.

"This is Millie San...Armati. I need a huge favor," she blurted out. "I need you to stall one of the ship's crewmembers, who is getting ready to board the ship. They'll be boarding in the next few minutes." She rattled off the crewmember's name. "Thanks. I owe you one, Suharto."

Millie shoved the phone in her pocket. "This will only buy us a few minutes. We're going to have to hustle."

To avoid being spotted, the women crossed back to the busy main thoroughfare. Cat and Millie jostled their way past the pedestrians and then ran the rest of the way to the security checkpoint.

A customs agent stationed at the entrance gate checked their ID's and then waved them through.

"I'm sure we beat her." Cat began walking toward the employee gangway.

"No." Millie shook her head. "We need to take the passenger gangway. It's closer to the medical center."

"You're right." Cat picked up the pace and Millie was hot on her heels as they raced toward the passenger gangway. Several passengers were in front of them and Millie kept glancing at her watch, praying they would hurry.

Finally, they were on the ship. Neither one slowed until they reached the medical center.

Cat pressed a hand to her chest, her face red from running in the heat. "Maybe it's a good thing we're here. I might be having a heat stroke."

"That's not funny." Millie slipped inside the medical center. "Doctor Gundervan?"

She could hear a rustling sound coming from the back and moments later, Doctor Gundervan emerged. "Are you two okay?"

"Yes. We need to get Dave Patterson down here right away," Millie said. "I think I know what happened to Tonya Rivera and I know who's been targeting Danielle."

"What does that have to do with me?"

"You'll see. I need to borrow a radio."

Gundervan grabbed the one off the desk and handed it to Millie. She radioed Patterson, asking him to meet her in the medical center, and telling him it was an emergency.

"Danielle needs to be here, too." Millie radioed her friend, asking her to meet her in the medical center.

Millie set the radio on the desk. All of the pieces were starting to fall into place. Tonya, who worked at the spa, picking up prescription drugs at the port. Rachel Quaid visiting the spa and Stephen Chow for acupuncture treatments, complaining of back pain.

"Does Rachel have back issues?" Millie directed her question at Gundervan.

"Not that I'm aware of."

"So you weren't aware she's been visiting the spa and specifically Stephen Chow with complaints of back pain?"

"No."

Patterson arrived and Danielle was right behind him. She took one look at Millie's dirt-stained face and started laughing. "What happened to you?"

"You look like you got caught up in a dust bowl," Patterson said.

Millie frowned. "No. Nic and I spent the day exploring the island on dune buggies and it was a little dirty."

"Shall we get to it?" Patterson asked.

Gundervan, Patterson and Danielle gazed at Millie expectantly.

"Well?" Cat prompted. "We have a captive audience."

"Rachel Quaid killed Tonya Rivera. The women were dealing prescription drugs, selling them to crewmembers and possibly even passengers."

Doctor Gundervan's mouth dropped open. "That's absurd," he sputtered. "I've never heard anything so ridiculous in my entire life. I believe you may be suffering from a heat stroke. And you…"

He turned accusing eyes on Cat. "You're behind this. You couldn't stand the thought Rachel and I are friends and now you're outright lying and making stuff up to try to get rid of her."

Cat looked horrified. "I did not. What Millie is saying is true. We saw it with our own eyes."

"Rachel is down at the gangway right now, trying to board the ship with some prescription drugs. I suspect she used one of the prescriptions from your prescription pad." Millie pointed to Gundervan. "To purchase the drugs."

"I…I don't believe it."

Patterson turned to Gundervan. "Is there a way to verify that?"

"Yes, of course. All of the prescriptions are numbered." Gundervan shot Cat a look of disgust before turning his attention to the medical center's laptop.

The others remained silent as he studied the screen. "The last prescription I wrote was 2798." He pulled a set of keys from his pocket, unlocked the top desk drawer, reached inside and pulled out a prescription pad.

Doctor Gundervan let out a sharp breath.

"The next one isn't 2799, is it?" Millie quietly asked.

"How did you know?" Gundervan whispered.

"I didn't figure it out until this afternoon. My guess is if you look back, you'll see a bunch of other missing prescriptions, all stolen by Rachel, who forged your signature to order more drugs."

Millie laid out her theory that Rachel and Tonya somehow partnered to start purchasing the drugs through either legitimate or even non-legitimate sources. Something happened, perhaps the two argued.

"Rachel slipped drugs into Tonya's drink or food and she overdosed," Millie said. "In a panic, Rachel attempted to set Danielle up by planting an empty prescription bottle in her jacket pocket. She took Tonya's keycard, planning to return to the cabin later to search for the drug money or missing drugs."

"So she was in my cabin searching for the missing drugs," Danielle theorized. "That's why she kept breaking in and even set up a camera."

"It's possible she suspected Danielle of being involved and perhaps even hiding the Miami delivery, but I was the one who intercepted it at the port last week," Patterson said.

"She may have also been the one who broke into the spa breakroom and searched Tonya's locker," Millie said. "My theory is Tonya was transferred from the Marquise of the Seas for disciplinary action, but not fired."

"She was," Patterson said. "A quick call to the pharmacy to check with the pharmacist will confirm our suspicions."

"What pharmacy?" Doctor Gundervan asked. "I'm sure there are dozens nearby."

"The name of the pharmacy is Port Square Pharmacy," Cat said.

Doctor Gundervan switched his cell phone on and tapped the screen. "I found it."

The others waited quietly while he dialed the number and asked to speak with the pharmacist. There was a short pause and Millie's heart began to race. What if she was wrong? How bad would it look if Rachel were innocently picking up a prescription for her bad back? Millie would be the laughingstock of the ship, or at least the security department.

"Hello. This is Doctor Joe Gundervan, on board the cruise ship the Siren of the Seas. My nurse, Rachel Quaid, was on her way to your pharmacy to pick up a prescription and I wondered if she'd showed up yet." Gundervan paused.

"I see. Yes, and the pharmaceutical brand?"

There was another pause. "Thank you for your time." Gundervan disconnected the call and set the phone on his desk. "Rachel picked up a prescription for oxycodone using my signature."

"A quick search when she returns will confirm our suspicions," Patterson said. "If it is Rachel, she would know enough not to run the packages through the scanner machine and would hide them somewhere on her body."

"I agree," Millie said. "The body scanners only detect metal or weapons. Someone could easily get through if they were concealing drugs."

"I thought she was having emotional issues and was trying to help," Gundervan said. "She was taking emergency breaks on port days, throwing me off schedule."

Millie thought of Cat, how hurt she was that Gundervan kept cancelling their dates at the last minute and now she knew why. It wasn't Gundervan…it was Rachel. "Don't you think you owe Cat an apology?"

Gundervan took a step toward Cat, but she wasn't having any of it. "I guess I know where we stand." She shot him a disgusted look and marched out of the medical center, slamming the door shut behind her.

"That went well," Patterson said. "Can't say as I blame Cat."

"I asked the gangway crew to detain Rachel. They can't keep her for long," Millie said. "I'm sure you would like to speak to her without us hanging around."

Danielle and Millie exited the medical clinic, and Danielle remained silent until they reached the stairwell. "Did you suspect it was Rachel all along?"

"At one point, I did kind of think Rachel might have been involved. The fact she had access to prescriptions, she was visiting with Stephen Chow and spending a lot of time in the spa area where Tonya worked." Millie admitted she suspected Camille, as well. "She put a lot of trust in Tonya by letting her sign for packages, even though Tonya had only been a spa employee for a short time."

"Don't forget about Arvin," Danielle said. "I thought he might be involved, especially after I caught him trying to sneak into the spa breakroom the other night."

"I'm sure Patterson is on top of that," Millie said. "I'm worried about Cat."

"Yeah." Danielle blew air through thinned lips. "She was furious, and who can blame her? Gundervan was acting like it was Cat's fault."

"That romance is definitely on the rocks." Millie didn't have time to dwell on Rachel's meeting with Gundervan and Patterson, or Cat and Gundervan's off-again relationship. She needed to return to work, but first, it was time for a much-needed shower.

Millie scrubbed every inch of her body and as she scrubbed, a slow smile lit her face. There was one more bright spot in Millie's day and she had no intention of letting it slip through her fingers.

Chapter 22

Millie couldn't wait to call Andy. "I'm back from my day off. I'll meet you at the gangway to greet the returning guests. I'm bringing your costume with me."

"What costume?" Andy asked.

"The costume you promised to wear if you lost the stinky scarecrow bet," Millie reminded him.

"You can't be serious."

"Oh. I am serious, Andy. A bet is a bet. Besides, the passengers will love your new look," Millie teased. She didn't give Andy a chance to argue and clipped the radio to her belt before slipping her work shoes on and heading down to the gangway.

Andy was already there greeting some of the returning guests. She held out the bag. "Here ya go."

"Millie, this is silly," Andy said.

"Is it?" Millie arched her brow. "It wasn't silly when you forced me to wear it the other day during the movie marathon."

"It was a fitting costume, perfect for the fall theme."

"And this is the perfect costume to fit in with your fall festivities and greet the guests." She motioned toward the costumed pirate standing at the bottom of the gangway ramp and posing for pictures with the passengers. "See? The passengers love to have their picture taken with costumed crew."

Andy's eyes widened in horror at the thought. "Do you think the passengers will want their picture taken with me, too?"

"Absolutely." Millie thrust the bag in his hand. "Now hop to it. Your adoring fans are waiting."

Andy opened his mouth to argue, but Millie firmly shook her head. "A bet is a bet."

"All right." Andy's steps dragged as he made his way to the elevator.

Millie kept one eye on the elevator doors and the other on the gangway to greet the returning passengers. She did a double take when the doors opened and Andy, the witch, stepped out.

She couldn't help herself and laughed so hard, tears began streaming down her cheeks. "I want a picture."

Millie pulled her phone from her pocket and switched it on as she slipped an arm around Andy. "Smile."

"No," Andy pouted. "This isn't funny."

"You're right. It's hilarious." She snapped a selfie of them and returned the phone to her pocket, anxious for the next round of passengers to make their way onto the ship. "Would you like your picture taken with Wicked Andy, the evil witch?" Millie asked.

"Oh yes." One of the women tottered over and peered at Andy's face. "Are you Andy the cruise director?"

"The one and only." Millie motioned for one of the cameramen to join them. "Can you hang out here for a little while? I think the passengers are excited to have their pictures taken with Andy the evil witch."

Millie had a lot of fun, encouraging all of the passengers to have their picture taken with Andy. Many of them declined, but each time she explained the witch was Andy, the cruise director, they changed their mind.

"You're popular, Mr. Walker," the cameraman said. "You should wear that costume more often. The passengers really like it."

"Over my dead body."

Finally, Andy had enough. "I kept my end of the deal." When he returned, he wasn't alone. Dave Patterson was with him. "You were right."

"It was Rachel," Millie said.

"Yes. When she returned to the medical center, I asked to search her packages. She had shoved the prescription in her pants pocket to avoid detection when going through security. At first, she denied everything. It wasn't until she found out Gundervan had talked to the pharmacist that she showed us the bottle of pills."

"Did Rachel confess to murdering Tonya?" Millie asked.

"Not at first. She admitted to forging a prescription."

"So she didn't admit to giving Tonya an overdose of drugs?"

"Not until I told her we had her on camera breaking into Danielle's cabin using Tonya's keycard."

"She denied it," Millie guessed.

"Yes. We searched Rachel's cabin and found the hoodie she was wearing the day you and Danielle caught her on tape inside the cabin."

"I knew it." Millie clapped her hands. "She was the one who set up the surveillance camera and the one who left the note 'you're next.'" She had another thought. "What about Arvin Kurtz? We spotted him snooping around the spa the other night."

"He claims he was in love with Tonya, was convinced someone had murdered her and was trying to figure out what happened."

"Perhaps you have another ship sleuth on your hands," Millie laughed.

"That's all I need. In the meantime, I'm already working on tracking down more forged prescriptions at pharmacies in the Miami area." Patterson shook his head. "I don't know how you do it."

"This time luck was on my side. Our next step was to set up a sting in Danielle's cabin to try to draw the intruder out. Spotting Rachel inside the pharmacy saved us the trouble. So you don't suspect that Arvin and Camille may have also been involved?" She didn't mention Stephen Chow's name.

"Rachel insists it was just the two of them, that no one else was involved." Patterson turned his attention to Andy. "I saw your cutesy witch costume. I thought that belonged to Millie."

"It did. I lost a bet," he said miserably. "Now my mugshot will be all over the ship and in thousands of pictures."

"You looked awesome," Millie said. "The passengers loved it."

"You shouldn't make bets with Millie," Patterson advised. "She's good."

"A little too good," Andy said. "You can stop gloating now or the next costume will be a Christmas elf."

"I like elves, better than wicked witches," Millie said. "I have to say I'll be surprised if you don't win your bet with Claudia."

"Thanks to you and the other crewmembers," Andy said. "We're not done yet. The fall festivities have only just begun. Which reminds me, I ordered a one-of-a-kind pumpkin prop I need you to sign for when we get to Miami on Saturday."

Millie rolled her eyes. "Oh no. Here we go again."

The end.

If you enjoyed reading "Deadly Delivery," please take a moment to leave a review. It would be greatly appreciated. Thank you.

The series continues...Book 15 in the "Cruise Ship Cozy Mysteries" series coming soon!

Books in This Series

Starboard Secrets: Book 1
Portside Peril: Book 2
Lethal Lobster: Book 3
Deadly Deception: Book 4
Vanishing Vacationers: Book 5
Cruise Control: Book 6
Killer Karaoke: Book 7
Suite Revenge: Book 8
Cruisin' for a Bruisin': Book 9
High Seas Heist: Book 10
Family, Friends and Foes: Book 11:
Murder on Main: Book 12
Fatal Flirtation: Book 13
Deadly Delivery: Book 14
Book 15: Coming Soon!
Cruise Ship Cozy Mysteries Box Set I (Books 1-3)
Cruise Ship Cozy Mysteries Box Set II (Books 4-6)
Cruise Ship Cozy Mysteries Box Set III (Books 7-9)

Meet the Author

Hope loves to connect with her readers! Connect with her today!

Never miss another book deal! Text the word Books to 33222

Visit **hopecallaghan.com/newsletter** for special offers, free books,
and soon-to-be-released books!

Pinterest:
https://www.pinterest.com/cozymysteriesauthor/

Facebook:
https://www.facebook.com/authorhopecallaghan/

Hope Callaghan loves to write mystery books, especially Christian Mystery and Cozy Mystery books. She has written more than 50 mystery books (and counting) in five series.

In March 2017, Hope won a Mom's Choice Award for her book, "Key to Savannah," Book 1 in the Made in Savannah Cozy Mystery Series.

Born and raised in a small town in West Michigan, she now lives in Florida with her husband.

She is the proud mother of one daughter and a stepdaughter and stepson. When she's not doing the thing she loves best - writing books - she enjoys cooking, traveling and reading books.

Pumpkin Crunch Cake Recipe

by Marcia Lamb

Ingredients:
1 - 29-oz can pumpkin
1 - 13-oz. can evaporated milk
1 cup sugar
3 eggs
1 tsp. cinnamon
1 box Duncan Hine's yellow cake mix
1 cup chopped nuts (pecan, walnuts or macadamia nuts)

(Frosting):
One 8-oz cream cheese softened
3/4 cup Cool Whip
3/4 cup powdered sugar

Cake Directions:
Mix pumpkin, evaporated milk, sugar, eggs and cinnamon.
Pour into 9x13 pan lined with wax paper.
Pour/sprinkle one box Duncan Hines' yellow dry cake mix on top of the batter. Spread around the whole top.
Sprinkle one cup of chopped nuts on top.
Bake at 350 degrees for 50 minutes.
After the cake cools, turn it over (out of pan)

Frosting Directions:
Blend cream cheese, Cool Whip and powdered sugar.
After cake has cooled, spread frosting over the top.

Made in the USA
Monee, IL
04 February 2021